YOU'RE
MINE
TONIGHT

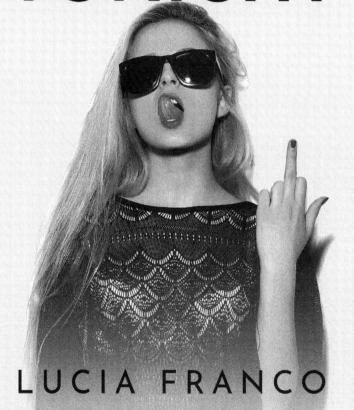

LUCIA FRANCO

You're Mine Tonight
Copyright © 2022 by Lucia Franco

Edited by Nadine Winningham
Proofread by Mattingly Churakos
Cover Design by Opulent Designs

All rights reserved. No part of this publication may be reproduced, distributed, or transmitted in any form or by any means, including photocopying, recording, or other electronic or mechanical methods, without the prior written permission of the publisher, except in the case of brief quotations embodied in critical reviews and certain other noncommercial uses permitted by copyright law.

This is a work of fiction. Names, characters, businesses, places, events and incidents are either the products of the author's imagination or used in a fictitious manner. Any resemblance to actual persons, living or dead, or actual events is purely coincidental.

ALSO BY
LUCIA FRANCO

People will stare.
Make it worth their while.

YOU'RE MINE TONIGHT

CHAPTER 1

Roxy

ENERGY VIBRATES AT THE TIPS OF MY FINGERS. A small audience fills the room; their electric buzz illuminates my body. I sway to the beat with a wistful happiness, flying high, my arms thrown in the air like every other girl in here feeling herself.

My best girlfriend, Estelle, grazes my hip as she dances to her own beat. When she found out the American rock band the Thirteenth Floor was set to play at the Sunset Den, she begged me to tag along with her. It's not that I would have said no. The lead singer is on her to-do list, and she hasn't even met him yet.

The superstition behind the bands name intrigues me. Fame has allowed me to stay in the best of the best hotels. Most of which do not have a thirteenth floor because it denotes bad luck.

After *A Luxe Life*, the reality television show Estelle and I were on, took pop culture by storm, we became a brand and didn't even know it. Cameras had recorded our every move and the world watched as we had the time of our lives. Each season had taken us to a new location, experiencing culture in ways we hadn't despite our rich upbringings. We were two freshly turned sixteen-year-old socialites at the time, both from prestigious backgrounds padded by wealth, both rebels without a cause, and complete strangers to one another. We had been thrown together to live among blue-collar people and attend their schools. I went from a private all-girl Catholic school in Brentwood, California, to farming my own vegetables in Tuscany and not attending school at all. It was a life-altering experience, one that brought my best friend into my life, and where I discovered a love for baking after filming in Italy.

Being born into money has its benefits. We get away with murder, and no one says a single thing.

It's been a couple of years since the show went into syndication. While I've made my own name for myself, all people see is Bardot Studios when they look at me . . . And not much else.

2

Which means they want something from me.

And indie bands always want something.

Show business runs in my blood dating back to my great-great-grandfather. Bardot Studios originated in a garage between two brothers who had their sights set on the Hollywood sign. Most people who come to California want to be in front of the camera. The Bardot brothers wanted to be behind it.

Now the family name is on everything in Los Angeles. It's like the six degrees of Bardot. Everyone in Hollywood can somehow be linked to the name.

"This is my favorite song of theirs," Estelle says, cheesing hard. She said that two songs ago.

The room darkens to the beat of the drums. I watch as hues of amber flash softly. The lead singer looks nothing like what one would imagine a rocker to look. He appears to be more of a timid college student whose nose is stuck between a physics book simply because he likes it. Like he'd be more comfortable in a library that's closed for the night instead of the nightclub we're currently in.

All that goes out of the window though once he opens his mouth. He's no longer a nerd. He's a sex god with soul, and I understand the appeal now. His voice is the kind that beckons ladies to drop to their knees while putting their hands up for more.

He's not my type, but I'm not dead either.

Los Angeles has jaded me. I guess that's what happens when you jet set through glitz and glamor with rose-colored glasses. My film producing parents saw nothing wrong with bringing me and my brother to their endless parties. I was smoking cigarettes by twelve and tossing back shots with my younger brother by thirteen. Goldschläger was the worst. At fourteen I was stealing prescription pills from my dad and breaking into my mom's wine collection to wash them down. I got grounded for drinking a vintage bottle of pinot grigio but not for drinking in general. My life is all sorts of fucked up. But that's the notorious lifestyle of Hollywood's darlings, and no one makes a fuss about it.

"Come on, Roxy. Let's get drinks and then head down there," Estelle suggests, and I nod, letting go of my past. "I want to see what my future ex-husband is like."

I chuckle. She's always looking for her next conquest. "I'm gonna get us a double," I tell her. There's always a waiter close by in the VIP section. I turn and motion to one with my chin.

Estelle's my partner in crime. We'd grown close during filming and felt more like sisters than friends. Thankfully the show had been a success, and we profited well enough to purchase a house together in the private gated community of Hidden Hills. We spent our first earnings on it and have lived there ever since.

Being a Bardot comes with benefits.

And addictions.

Turning my attention back to the stage, I tune into the song, immediately liking the weightier melody. My body is humming with something I can't put my finger on. The lyrics are a sinful desperation, and the voice weakens my knees. His sorrow speaks to me.

My focus shifts to the shirtless piano player. He's telling a story without having to open his mouth. I watch as he strikes the keys with persuasive tenderness, the notes echoing through my chest. He leans in close to the instrument, and I squint. A vein throbs across a strip of his throat. I bet he's slick with those fingers. I wonder what he can do with them.

"He looks bang worthy," I say to Estelle without looking at her. "Would that make us groupies if we both hook up with guys from the same band tonight?" When she doesn't respond, I look over my shoulder and do a double take. I'm speaking to the waiter and not my best friend.

"Oh!" I jump, and laughter explodes from me. "I didn't see you there." Confusion mars the space between his brows as he stares back at me. "Can we get a double shot of tequila, please? Salt, lime, and a body to lick it from." I give him a once over, then meet his gaze. "Preferably yours."

"When I'm off the clock, it's yours." *Nice,* I think to myself. He's pretty cute, and he could totally be my late-night snack. "And yeah, that makes you groupies," he adds. "You and every other female in this room are trying to bone the lead singer. Get in line because they're all after him tonight."

My gaze shoots to Estelle. "I take that as a challenge, don't you?" She nods, and I glance back at the waiter and smile. "There's a first time for everything, I guess."

He's gone and back before the song is over, handing

us our shots with shaky fingers. Clear liquid spills over the edge.

That was quick. I almost want to check his pants to see if he's got a boner.

"I love a good rim rocker." I emphasize my words. "Thanks, lover," I say, but he doesn't leave.

The waiter looks right at me and says, "I bet you've never licked another man's asshole before. I can tell by looking at you that you haven't."

My eyes light up with a rebuttal. He's fun.

"Last month I blew my agent for some coke, then I showed him my thanks by having him bend over while I rocked his rim with my tongue and gave him a reach around with my hand." When the waiter doesn't reply, I add, "I snorted lines he poured out on his cock, then washed down the drip with his cum."

One wild and crazy night our mutual agent, Von, had been at the same party Estelle and I were paid to be at. He's a dirtbag at heart but can spew laws like he's a jailhouse attorney, just the kind of guy we need on our team in La-La Land. I'm convinced his wife is a mail-order bride from Russia. It's the only logical way he found some idiot willing to marry him. The man has an anaconda hanging between his legs and is addicted to sex.

I can't stand my agent, but he sure knows how to give a good dick ride.

"I watched the whole thing," Estelle says brazenly.

"When she finished, I decided to see what else he could be milked for."

A grin spreads across my face. She's telling the truth. Hollywood is seedy, but having a bestie who covers your six makes it worth it. The waiter leaves, shaking his head. He looks appalled.

"I got lint in my nose doing that," I say, recalling that moment.

I had been nice with the reach around, but I made him put a condom on before I got down on my knees. The last thing I needed was herpes simplex A thru Z because he couldn't keep his Johnson in his pants.

Did I ever think there'd come a day I'd be snorting coke from my agent's cock because I couldn't get ahold of my dealer?

Most definitely not.

But Von had agreed before he could blink, so I made him pour out a thick rail and went to town. I gave him a blow job despite how numb my mouth was from the powder.

I do not recommend blowies after numbing your gums. It tastes disgusting on top of feeling like I slobbered everywhere. All I could think about was his wife sucking his dick next and wondering why her husband's cock tasted like cocaine.

Like ninety-five percent of Hollywood, Von's an addict. We wanted what he had one night and since Scooter was MIA doing God knows what, we got down on our knees like good little girls and took turns blowing our agent in return for drugs. Von is known to have a smorgasbord of drugs. He can afford it with the millions he makes a year off my face and countless other celebrities.

Fucking Scooter. Resident drug dealer. Resident ghost face. I made sure to hit him up before we made it to the club tonight. Estelle wanted to party, so I brought the goods.

Scooter sells to everyone when he's not making dope beats for the music world. He's a modern-day Eminem with the ability to construct a melody and lyrics way ahead of his time. Scooter can't rap though. He's total shit at it. He's a straight behind the scenes guy, and that's all he'll ever be.

Celebrities, film producers, CEOs of Fortune 500 companies, anyone who works in Hollywood knows Scooter on a first name basis. He has connections low and high and can get anything off the streets or locked away in pharmacies. It's how he became a household name in the Hills.

"Let's take the shots and then go scope out our next mistake."

We clink our glasses, then shoot back the second shot of tequila like it's water.

Hollywood, California, is nothing more than a festering, bleeding love affair. I pray I make it to see twenty-eight breathing on my own.

CHAPTER 2

Roxy

'M STARTING TO FEEL GOOD. *REALLY GOOD.*

Time blends with the colors we're dancing through. Our glasses end up on the hand carved black cherry wood table we're sitting at in the exclusive VIP section. I do a double take and focus on the center of the table that's been divided in two. It looks like someone cut a tree down in their backyard with an axe, then put it back together with clear glitter glue. I get lost in the crimson river that flows through the center like a private valley. It looks like glass, but I can't tell. The beautiful shimmer captivates me. Inhaling deeply, I release a sigh as warmth coats my veins and the alcohol heightens my senses.

Reaching into my Channel crossover purse, Estelle watches closely as I take out a rectangle compact and flip the top back. She hums in anticipation and a drug-induced smile spans her face. Estelle's just as bad with partying as I am. Usually I keep the rocks in a glass vial, but I crushed them in advance and poured it into a dime bag. She's already moving and peels back the paper of a new straw left on the table, then she digs into the kit on my lap and takes out the mini scissors I stole from my seamstress and cuts two small, clean straws.

I'm an addict, but I come with standards. You'll never catch me snorting lines from the lid of a public toilet. Feces, anyone? A rolled-up dollar bill falls into the same category. That may be worse than a toilet lid.

And don't get me started on the fingernail bump. Hands are filthy in general, and cleanliness is next to godliness.

I flick the bag with my middle finger and give it a good shake before opening it. Estelle leans over and sticks her straw into a corner of the bag. She holds her other nostril shut before she snorts the cocaine with a deep breath. More than half the bag goes straight to her brain.

I mock gawk at her. "You're like a Hoover fucking vacuum, you know that?"

Her eyes squeeze shut as she tilts her head back, and she shoves the coke toward me. She gags next, then sniffles and swallows thickly. The straw kinks in her hand. I snort the other corner as she recovers, tasting it almost immediately in the back of my throat. Exhilaration prickles every nerve in my body despite the gnarly taste. Pleasure crawls over my skin like I'm wrapped up in a blanket of heat. Instant gratification beams straight to my core and ignites a needy desire through my blood.

I stick the baggie back in my tin, and tuck it away for later.

The band's set changes, and the tinted lights drop low. A golden hue illuminates the red shadows of the room now. It adds a touch of sensuality to the air that softens the senses and puts me on cloud nine. A waiter strolls by and I pluck a shot off the tray he's carrying. Estelle does the same.

I bring the glass to my lips and tip it back. Between the shots and coke, I can't feel the burn anymore.

Turning around, we bump into each other as we move to the rhythm of the music. An electric guitar screams through the speakers and the drums beat inside my chest. I look toward the stage and notice the moody guitarist jamming out in his own world. There's a larger crowd now, and Estelle is next to me swaying to the music as she stares at the lead singer like she's ready to bust out a kid for him.

My gaze lands on the man leaning against the wall behind the stage. He's engaged in his phone more than the show's finale. His shoulder is pressed against the wall and his legs are crossed at the ankles. He's wearing dark wash jeans, a light grayish Henley, and a pair of dark combat boots.

It's not typical nightclub attire for West Hollywood, which makes me think he's here with the band.

Dirty blond hair falls around his facial scruff. He's as casual as it comes with the swag of a rogue. He looks out of place standing there alone, but it doesn't seem to bother him in the least.

And I kind of like that.

A few of the buttons on his shirt are undone at his throat. The black walls behind him exude edginess, casting the stranger in a fume of burning smoke. I find myself staring at him, oddly intrigued. Tawny lighting accentuates his muscular frame. I wish I could see his eyes, but he's too far away.

Something about him ignites a glow inside of me the more I observe him while I dance with Estelle. My eyes drop, following his sudden movement as he reaches down to adjust his cock. I watch him bend at the knees next to loosen his sack like it's sticking to him. He goes back to texting on his phone, unaware I'm eyeing his every move. He fills out his jeans too well, and for a split second I wonder if he's a lumber jack.

I become parched. He's ruggedly handsome and looks like a strong man. I have the sudden urge to get on my knees and taste him, a bizarrely odd thought that takes me by surprise. I've never looked at a man before and felt such a need. I'd rather them get on their knees for me, but he stirs something inside of me I've never felt until now. I rake a gaze down the length of his body and like what I see. A shot of desire licks through my veins. My body calls out to him like a summoning.

I need to walk over and get his name. The man has broad shoulders and he's what would be considered barrel chested. He's hefty but not steroid hefty, which I appreciate. Any guy who injects steroids reduces the size of his cock by a quarter inch. And we can't have that.

"My night just got a bit more interesting," I singsong to my bestie.

Estelle turns and follows my gaze, dancing with me as she studies him. I wish he would look at me. The song playing in the background fades to almost nothing and the band says something to the crowd, but I'm not listening. The stranger picks up his head like he's paying attention, and that's when I lose all air in my lungs.

He's ridiculously handsome. The kind of man who exudes masculinity like he was born with it on his skin but isn't aware of it. He doesn't look cocky, but he totally rocks a "don't disturb me" vibe, which entices me more. I can't tear my eyes from this beautiful stranger and the aura he's putting off.

His eyes fall in a downward sloop and accidently meet mine. He blinks, turning his head in my direction, and immediately does a double take.

A gasp hitches in my throat.

He captures my stare, and it throws me off balance. I can't stop staring, which I know is rude, but I have all of this man's attention and I like the way it feels. I wanted him to look at me, and now that he is, I'm unexpectedly shy by the intensity in his gaze. My dancing slows to a sway. I eye him over my shoulder, attempting to move to the rhythm of the music, pretending not to notice him but doing a piss-poor job of it.

He hasn't looked away. He pushes off the wall with his shoulder, then reaches behind him to pocket his cell phone before he's striding away, his gait thick with determination. I like how he walks, like he's on a mission. My stomach tightens with anticipation. I hope he's coming toward me.

He makes his way around the stage and walks directly across the dance floor. Someone bumps into him, but it doesn't faze him. My heart is thumping wildly the closer he grows. I take a small step back.

All these ridiculous scenarios pop into my head of what he could do next, and I desperately want to be part of them. My breathing deepens. I take another unsteady foot back and bump into Estelle. This man is insanely gorgeous with a roughness around him that speaks to me, and he's headed my way.

He draws closer and my lips part as I look into a pair of hypnotizing eyes. The kind that one would get lost in. The kind of eyes that hold more than they give.

The kind that makes me want to be bad.

He peers down his nose that looks like it's been broken a time or two. We don't know each other, but I go straight into his arms without a thought and dance with him. He presses his hard body to mine and holds me like I'm his.

Large hands skim my hips as goose bumps weave up my spine.

I take a deep breath, then release a soft sigh. He doesn't seem intimidated by my height or curvy figure, and that only increases his chances of sealing the deal with me. He wedges one leg between mine, moving to my rhythm. We dirty dance too well together, fitting like a puzzle piece. He's got one arm fastened around my lower back, the other moving higher between my shoulder blades to grip the back of my neck. The pads of his fingers dig into my skin, the pressure of my pulse increasing where his thumb is. It should scare me, he's a stranger, but it doesn't.

It only makes me burn for him more.

"Who are you?" he asks, swaying with me.

"You don't know who I am?"

"I don't."

"I find it hard to believe you don't know me."

Blue eyes penetrate mine. I like how he looks at me, like he's thinking hard about what he wants to say next.

"I'm not into sex tapes. Porn is for amateurs."

A grin breaks out across my face. His dislike for porn catches me by surprise. It's impossible to stop the laughter from flowing past my lips.

"It's not often you hear a man hates porn."

"I don't hate it. I can just do it better." He shrugs casually and I almost fucking purr.

"Not when it's two women. It can be erotic watching them have sex while you do."

His lips purse, uncaring. "You know what else is erotic? My tongue inside your pussy while I suck the orgasm from your cunt. I won't stop until I get every drop from you. Not until your thighs are shaking and you're about to kick me in the head because your clit needs a break from my teeth. Porn doesn't compare to eating pussy. I bet yours tastes like warm sugar."

I blink rapidly, unable to find words. While I wouldn't know what my pussy tastes like, I can tell you it's wet and about to drip down my thigh. What he said was hot as hell.

Still not better than porn, though.

"Like a warm donut," I say, correcting him.

His gaze lowers and his nostrils flare. He brazenly skims his hand under my dress to cup my ass. He tugs me closer, getting adjusted, and his hips shift into mine. My stomach dips as his erection presses on my pussy. It jerks. Heat flares through my blood and our connected gaze deepens. I've never been so caught off guard and turned on at once. I want to take his hand and shove it between my thighs and say "yes, please."

He continues, and I'm dumbstruck he has more to say.

"When I finally do grant you mercy, it'll only be to turn you over so I can fuck whatever hole I'm in the mood for like you owe me."

My brow raises at the thought. His crooked front teeth drag over his bottom lip I'm suddenly thirsty to taste. His words provoke a spicier side of me I didn't know I had. I've envisioned being manhandled and taken like it's my fucking duty, but it's never actually happened. And I've never heard any of my gal friends mention it either.

I'm a thicker woman. I've yet to have a man who can toss me around like I'm a rag doll. Usually I have to do the work myself and assume the position. Where's the fun in that?

"I must be doing something right if you can't talk."

I finally regain myself. I kind of want to see if he could bend me like a Barbie. What he says and what I have in mind is too hot for a porno, that's for sure.

I lick my lips, and he follows my tongue with a heady stare. "Most men don't have the goods to back it up. Nothing I haven't heard before, playboy."

"You're not satisfied," he states.

Typical of him to assume that. "I am actually. Often."

"Not often," he corrects. "I can read between the lines. Having sex with yourself doesn't count, and it sure as fuck doesn't give you an orgasm the way a real cock can."

I like the way his eyes penetrate mine, like he's trying to figure me out because he's curious. He's a drum humming to my soul. It makes me want to put my money where his mouth is.

"Maybe I'll take both," he adds, and I swear I feel his erection twitch at the center of my hips. "I bet your ass looks gorgeous with a cock inside of it. Two sugarplum ass cheeks bouncing on my cock."

I swallow thickly. My mind is racing with visions I've only dreamed about. Erotic, sweaty bodies instantly fill my head with fantasies. I've never allowed any man back there for a few reasons. But this nameless stranger who causes the pounding in my heart to escalate with each passing second makes me want to throw my morals out of the window.

"I bet your ass jiggles like a ripple of water when you hit that peak and need to ride hard and fast to get that orgasm out. Mmm. Show me you want to fuck me the way I'm gonna fuck you and you'll never look for another cock again."

My brows raise. "I'm not sure I like the idea of my body being equated to cellulite."

"Women," he mumbles under his breath like he's offended. "You don't understand. That's not what I see when my cock is being pumped by your cunt. I don't know a single guy to ever talk shit about a fat ass other than to say how good it feels to be deep inside one."

"I bet you tell all the girls that," I say, batting my lashes in a dramatic effect. "Do they fall at your boots and whine to be taken by a big burly man like yourself?" My breathing is labored but not too much to flirt with him. Drawing on the years of acting I have under my belt, I pretend to be a lonely, desperate housewife and look up at him with little doe eyes. "My husband doesn't pay attention to me. Fuck me, please. And then you proceed to say all the hottest things you could come up with like you have a one-stop cock shop."

He laughs, and he reminds me of a bear in hibernation. My mouth twitches as I attempt to stop the smirk teasing my lips. He's not impressed with my antics, and it makes me want to giggle.

I'm not sure what's happening with my thoughts or where his filthy mouth came from, but all I know is that I'm worked up for this guy and feeling ridiculously desired in his arms after a few colorful words.

"You can't skip first base," I tell him. "I won't allow it. How one kisses is how one fucks. And if I don't like the way you kiss, you're not getting under this dress."

"What if I'm in the mood to smash to some R&B music after a few blunts and the next night we fuck it out to tequila because we argue over some dumb shit. You're gonna judge me on a kiss? Game on. That just means I get to fuck you more than once."

My thighs tighten at the erotic thought that bursts through my mind. I think back to the words he said moments ago and imagine his tongue between my legs. I look at his mouth and imagine it between my thighs, his tongue burrowed deep enough inside me that his chin tickles my ass while he sucks my pleasure like he's thirsty for it. He wouldn't stop as I come either, like most men do. He'd make it his personal responsibility to see it through to the end and let me fuck his face without reserve. Because he wants me to. He'd let me have any desire I want, and I wouldn't feel guilty for it like it's wrong.

Subliminal thoughts brought us to this inevitable moment. I'm feeling depraved for something edgy, and I want him to give it to me. I decide I'm going to make him mine for the night.

"I don't usually fuck the same guy twice," I tell him without an ounce of guilt.

His brows shoot up, but he isn't buying it. "Oh, big balls Betty here won't eat leftover dick for breakfast."

"Faces to ride and people to see."

His head falls back and a burst of laughter expels from an incredible smile I didn't expect to see from him. I find myself staring at his mouth, wanting to say something witty to see him do that again, but nothing comes to mind. My chest melts into him more comfortably than I care to admit. I like what I see, and I like what I feel.

"The only leftovers worth having again is lasagna. No man compares to that."

All I can do is look at him. His nostrils flare as he works to suppress the lethal grin curling the corners of his lips.

"Put your arms around my neck," he demands. When I do, he asks, "Who are you?"

I forgot we hadn't exchanged names yet.

"Your worst nightmare."

"Sounds more like my fucking fantasy," he states, his eyes dropping to my mouth.

His thumb strokes my neck and I inhale, drawing him into me. A soft moan of approval trembles in the back of my throat as his fingers thread my nape and wrap the long strands of my hair around his knuckles. He tugs, and I groan.

"What is it that you want?" I find myself asking.

"You," he says without hesitation. "Your thighs wrapped around my neck, my tongue in your pussy. Your mouth on my cock as you choke." He slides his hand to my butt cheek and gives it a good squeeze. "Your ass cheeks in the air, primed and ready for me to burry my face in."

I swallow thickly. I really want to kiss him.

It's not normal for men to be this forward. Now I wish more would. His words make me feel wanted, sexy, and that makes me want to give him what he wants.

"Still trying to skip first base."

"Tell me why you want to kiss me."

"I want to see how good that mouth of yours works."

"My kind of first base requires my mouth on your tits and no audience." He pauses to ask again, "What's your name?"

"Is this the part where I say 'yours' and then you take me to your cave and ravish me all night?"

His mouth is on mine before I have a chance to blink.

My eyes fall shut and my arms tighten around his neck.

Yes.

I bring him closer as he holds me like we're reaching to breathe in the same air. His wide hands are splayed possessively on my body, moving all over my tight clothes like he needs to touch my skin. Needing more, I thrust my lips and push my tongue into his mouth, forcing him to open. He hooks the tip of his tongue around mine and tugs me in, taking complete control like he was waiting for me to make the move, fusing our mouths together.

He sucks on my tongue like one would give head, and it sends a shot of desire straight to my pussy. It's an oddly erotic pull in my blood. I moan wildly into his mouth before he's kissing me with a vigor that sends chills down my spine. Teeth nip mine. He's aggressive, demanding. I take a step back and then match his tenacity and show him I can kiss just as good too.

If a man can make me wet from kissing him, then I know he'll be good in the sack.

And he's got me dripping.

CHAPTER 3

Roxy

I T'S HARD TO BREAK AWAY FROM HOW HE'S GRINDING against me and fucking my mouth with his.

He's trying to prove a point, and I'm okay with that because he's good at it.

Breaking the kiss, I blink a few times to catch my breath. He looks confused. Shadows cast over his moody face. He's straining against the material of his jeans and the thought makes me hot imagining his cock like that. I want to feel him in my hands before I unzip him, that first touch of warmth when I stick my hand in his pants. *I need him now* is all that's coursing through my mind, but I don't want an audience either.

I bring my lips to his ear and whisper, "Follow behind me." His hands hold my hips, trying to still me like he wants to ask questions, but we don't have time for questions when I'm chasing an orgasm.

Estelle isn't far. We never stray from one another unless we give the signal. She senses me and turns her head. "It's for the book," I tell her as we air kiss each other. It's our signal to let the other know we're okay to part ways. It's something we came up with living alone and hitting the nightlife scene in Hollywood. The buddy system always wins.

I take him to the second floor and make a beeline for one of the private rooms, determined to jump on him the second I get him on the couch. He's hot on my trail and I realize that I want to put a name to his brutishly attractive face.

"What's your name?" I ask.

I pull him into a different room than the one I was in earlier with Estelle. I push him down on a chaise lounge, then I close the door.

"Now you want to exchange names. When we're alone?" he says from behind me. "Brody."

Doing a double take, I make sure the curtain swayed closed after the door closed to secure us. I don't mind a little audience from time to time but not when I'm already on the edge of my seat and it's the damn paparazzi watching.

"Brody," I repeat under my breath. "I like to know whose dick it is before I suck it."

The thought makes me wet talking to him like this. I whip off my purse and drop it to the floor next to the chair, then I hike up my dress to my hips. Brody's eyes darken.

"Sucking my dick isn't the only thing you'll be doing, but it's a start. Now get over here and give me that ass."

I can't move fast enough.

Straddling the chair, he anticipates my movements and leans forward to reach for me. My gaze drops to the center of his pants for a fleeting moment and I notice his bulge. I'm dying to see what his dick looks like. The desire streaming through my veins overrides any sensible thought. I move over his hips and then sink down on to him.

"It'll be in your mouth soon enough," he says, the prick that he is.

"Hopefully that's not the only place it'll be."

We meet halfway and my chest tightens as we come together, our limbs tangle around each other like we ache for the same kind of hunger. I'm taller than him now and usually I don't like towering over a man, but when he looks up and his peppery aroma envelopes me in a wave of heady desire, it reeves up my craving for him. He looks like he wants to worship me.

Grinding my pussy against him, I roll my hips over his, wishing I had no panties on. Wetness seeps from me and I suck in a breath, reeling in the pleasure floating through my veins. I'm tingling from need. My lips fall open and his eyes shoot to mine. His hand snakes between our bodies. I lift up on my knees to give him access just in time for him to slide my panties aside and drive two fingers into my aching pussy. I sink down on his hand and feel the warmth spread around us. His thumb grazes my swollen folds and I gasp, seeing stars. I clench around his digits and grip the back of his head.

"Whose cunt is this?" he asks, moving the fingers inside of me, his voice low.

My lips fall open to speak but nothing comes out. He presses his thumb to my little bundle of nerves and asks, "Whose clit is this? Whose pussy is gushing in my hand right now?"

My toes curl and my thighs quiver. Brody rubs my clit faster and I can't think clearly. I'm trying to say my name, but nothing is coming out of my mouth except moans. Unable to stop myself, I rub my pussy shamelessly on him and catch the faint sound of wetness sticking together.

"Goddamn, you're soaked," he grits out. "It's going to make me blow quicker than I want."

My hips pump against his palm and I'm beginning to feel bashful but at the same time I can't stop.

"Your pussy spread wide open on my palm," he says, getting off on it himself. He's letting me do what I want, and it feels divine. "Tell me your name and I'll make you come harder than you ever have."

"Is that a promise?"

He captures my mouth with his. He's letting me slow ride his hand while he kisses me with matching intensity. Just as my hips roll forward, he bends his fingers inside of me and curls his hand up to grip my mound like he's holding me. I'm at the mercy of a stranger. He's got a grip on my most intimate parts and it makes me break out in a shiver. It hurts yet feels so damn good as my clit throbs for release. I let go of his kiss and my head tilts back in ecstasy. He doesn't stop and drags his tongue along the roof of my mouth and down the sides, finishing with him nibbling on my lip.

"God, I wanna fuck you," he admits, thrusting his hips into mine. "The second I saw you, I wanted to rip your dress off and get inside of you."

His voice is like gravel. I finally answer him. "Roxy. My name is Roxy."

"Roxanne," he mutters under his breath. He grips my pussy tighter while repeating my name. It sounds like a sorrowful song on his lips. "I love a shaved pussy like yours," he says, gently stroking my bare mound. "It's soft, like it's been untouched."

My breathing labored, I need to feel him. I can't take it any longer.

I reach between us and undo his button and zipper in one swift move, then I shove my hand in his pants to get a feel for him. Brody groans the instant I palm his cock. I spread my fingers and reach for the tip, dragging my fingertip over the top. It's my favorite part of the male anatomy. I like feeling it pulsate under my touch and seeing the little purple veins strain. Brody bites down on his lip and peers into my eyes.

"Commando. So typical for you Hollywood heartthrobs."

Still, I stroke his strained erection and reach for his sack, wanting to feel him in my hand before I release him. I hum in satisfaction at the feel of his skin. His testicles rub together in my palm. I love sex and all that it entails.

"I don't do it to be cool."

"Oh yeah?"

"I do it because it makes my cock stay hard. I like to rock on the threshold of pleasure. It's what keeps me going. Have you ever tried it?"

I shake my head. I'm all for freeing the puss, just on my own terms, and not where someone can see it so casually.

I gotta have some standards.

My eyes zero in on his thick cock standing tall. I'm suddenly hungry to taste it but more so to feel it inside of me. I hold his rigid shaft to my pussy and take control, spreading myself open to rub my clit on his heat. My body lights up like an inferno, the indulgence too good to deny. Brody nestles us closer. Our moans are guttural and instant. We both want this, to stay lost in the delectable friction we've created. Need seeps down my inner thigh. I need more. I need him to . . .

"Fuck me already," I say aloud before I can stop myself. "Give me that orgasm you swore by. You're already talking too much."

He grabs my jaw and his dark gaze falls to my lips. The tip of his cock beads a drop of precum, and I use it to spread over the meaty head. He groans in delight, his hips rolling against mine in a seductive wave. I want to slide down on him and take his cock like I deserve it.

He nods his head, but he doesn't move. His intentions only get me more excited. "You got a mouth on you. Anyone ever tell you that?"

"Yeah, every other fucking guy I meet."

CHAPTER 4

Roxy

HIS EYES DARKEN.

A smile spreads across my face. He doesn't like hearing I've been with other men. It's in the way his body hardens that gives him away.

"Pull your top down and give me those tits."

Brody opens his mouth and waits while one of his hands skims my hips and wraps around my ass cheek to hold me in place.

"Take them out if you want 'em."

I challenge him, and I don't know why. His fingers glide

down the material of my thong. He rips it off so the elastic is left around my hips, then in quick succession, he hikes me up by the back of my thighs and thrusts me forward. I lose my balance and grab for the headrest of the chair. Brody leans back. His muscular thighs hold me in place and cause my hips to widen. Before I can blink, his mouth wraps around my breast, his tongue quickly searching for my nipple. He bites down to hold me in place then uses his other hand to reach around and blindly feel for my pussy. He taps it rapidly and the sound echoes through the small, intimate room. I'm exposed in the most vulnerable way, at his mercy, and all it does is make me burn hotter for him.

I hiss as Brody bites harder, trying to get his tongue down my top. Quickly I shove the flimsy strap aside and give him what he wants. My double D's bared in his face.

"Should've listened to me," he says with my throbbing nipple between his teeth.

"Still not walking the walk . . ."

Palming the back of his head, I smash his face into my breast. Brody's eyes fall closed and he draws in a deep breath as he sucks my nipple like he's drinking nectar from it. Desire causes my toes to curl and I reach for his cock again, but fail when Brody flattens his hand against my pussy and drags it toward my ass. My thoughts leave my brain when his skilled finger vibrates over my clit until my legs are quaking. God, I need to come already.

Without warning, his palm comes down and slaps my wide-open pussy. A little squeak escapes my lips and my hips rush forward. He slaps me again while he tongues my nipple and holds my hips in place with his strong arms. He knows it hurts.

"You ass," I say, somewhere lost between pleasure and pain. He does it again and my deceitful body responds to him.

"Tell me you don't like it."

I nod quietly. I do though.

I pull down the other strap of my dress and offer him the other breast. My hips rear back, wanting him to at least stick his finger in me again, but he doesn't. He moves my dress and I'm thankful the room we're in is so private. There's only one window and it's covered with a crushed velvet curtain.

With both hands, he massages my ass cheeks until my knees weaken and my pussy is all but reaching for his cock. He won't give it to me. It's like he's keeping it at arm's length, and it's only making me want it more. My legs shake and I'm forced to release my weight on him, something I was trying to avoid since I'm not built like a pixie the way most of Tinseltown is. I'm comfortable in my skin. I love my body and who I am. But not everyone is comfortable with me.

He releases my nipple with a pop, then opens his mouth and reaches for mine. He kisses me with a ferocity I know is real. This guy wants me. All of me. I know he does, and it makes me lose all inhibitions with him. Unable to take any more, I hike a knee up and align my hips with his. He shifts to give me what I want. I grab his mouth and hold his face to mine, kissing him senselessly while I rub myself furiously up and down his shaft.

"This is what I wanted to feel, right here," he says against my mouth. I grind my clit down on his shaft, and he helps me do it harder. I sigh in divine pleasure. "A nice ass in my hands and a warm pussy begging to ride me. Nothing feels better than the real thing though, and with your skin against mine like this, it makes the blood rush to my cock faster. Your pussy lips are suctioned to my dick. Show me how you want it and I'll give it to you."

"Oh yeah, playboy? Think you could handle me? I'm the whole package and I want what I want."

He leans in and takes a bite of my shoulder. "I bet you would let me fuck you raw right now if I wanted to."

I answer honestly. "Probably."

Brody's holding on to my hips so tight that I know he likes what he feels. His precum is all over my stomach. The slippery seed is sticky between us. It makes me want to bend down and lick his tip.

I love sex too much sometimes. The dirtier, the better, and the image of us right now is making me ridiculously wet. Each of us has a degenerate side only few can feed.

His fingers skim my body like he's hungry. Tension radiates through me to give him what he wants but to find release too. His fingers enter my pussy, then he uses the wetness to rub over my little hole. My eyes roll shut as he touches the forbidden area and applies pressure. I wilt against him, clenching my thighs with a sigh.

"What if I wanted to take you back here tonight? Would you let me?"

He grunts, trying to breech the hole. I rear my hips back, answering him. It's not that I'm against it . . . I just haven't had anal sex that I liked, and I rather test the waters with something a little less intrusive.

"Whatever you want," I find myself saying, rubbing myself down his shaft until I feel his tight sack slide against my pussy. It's not like we'd go straight to anal anyway. I need his cock inside of me before he tries anything else. His testicles massage against me. I moan at the pleasure wracking my body. "Just take me already. I'm yours."

Brody groans, his teeth gnashing into mine. Our limbs are tangled around one another, an ache so deep that we're both trying to sate so we hold on a little longer. His pelvis thrusts into me. Nails threaten to break my skin. Our kisses fight for the other, like an unspoken need asking to be filled. His kiss alone makes me forget my name. I can't recall a time when I was so freely wrapped in another man's arms and our sexes found heaven without having to enter it first.

"We ain't fuckin' just yet. Give me your lips and don't stop kissing me. The moment you stop is the moment I stop."

I swallow thickly. The subtle black vanilla of his cologne envelopes me. Shouldn't be too hard.

My teeth roll over my bottom lip before I dive in and kiss him. I love how his tongue battles for mine.

"That's it, babe," he mutters, encouraging me. My chest

tingles with delight. "Use my cock and fuck yourself. I know that's what you were doing before. Bet you never rubbed a dildo this good on your pussy."

"Brody, no, God, you feel incredible." My cheeks flare with embarrassment, but I don't hold back. His dick is too hard and too thick to stop. "I've never had a man speak to me like this."

"It turns you on, doesn't it?" I nod, sighing. He says, "Use me. You won't hurt me. Ride me without riding me. You do your thing, but I get to do mine."

The thought alone makes me almost orgasm. "Yes," is all I can say before I'm tackling his mouth and giving him what I can. I need to orgasm just to take the edge off at this point.

Brody doesn't wait and inserts two fingers from behind into my pussy. Thank fuck, I think, and show him how thankful I am. I clench around him instantly and hitch my leg up a little higher to give him more room. He makes sure to drag his fingers so I feel each ridge with the more pressure he applies. He's manipulating my inner walls and stretching me out while his other hand can't stop gripping my ass. One of his fingers breaches the puckered hole and I'm moving rapidly over him.

"Relax," he says between my frantic kisses and slows me down with his strong arms. "It won't hurt." He pushes past the burning rim while pumping his other fingers into my pussy saying, "That's it. Loosen up and let me get you off right."

I do as he says and let the rest of my inhibitions go if we're going this far. I try not to think about anything other than the fact that he's got a finger in my ass and two fingers in my pussy, his tongue nearly in my throat. There's an immense amount of pleasure radiating through me. My fingers thread his hair and I pull on it at the scalp, fighting the urge inside of me not to ride him like an untamed horse. Brody works my pussy so good that I bring his mouth to my nipples again and ask him to suck them both.

"I know you said not to stop, but I'm so close and I want your mouth on my nipples when I come on you."

I don't know what's gotten into me.

"You come kissing me or you don't come at all. I get your orgasm."

I whimper. He makes it so difficult. "Just one little lick?" I ask.

Brody pushes his finger as deep as my ass will let him. I tighten and my eyes roll shut just as his mouth connects with my hardened nipple and he tongue fucks it. My hips are on autopilot as the orgasm climbs to the point of no return. His fingers move at a different speed that sends a rocket of shivers over me. I feel like I'm on a teetering seesaw.

The orgasm gets close, and I know I have to pull my tits back to kiss him, but the pleasure is so divine that I don't want to. I'm close to seeing stars.

"Ah, ah, ah, Brody."

My head falls back and I arch like a porn star, not caring at this point while I chase that high. I can't wait to fuck him next if this is how I feel from some foreplay. Brody releases my breast, and my hips vibrate like I just turned on one of my toys. My toes curl and desire finally consumes me when he says, "Get that dick, girl. Your clit is gonna leave a mark on me."

My fingers thread his hair and I kiss him roughly. I ride him like I'm on a mission out of hell and cry in relief as I pretty much hump his dick. I come hard, shaking. He manages to hit every erogenous zone I have and it sends me into a tizzy without actual dick penetration.

"You like the idea of marking my cock, don't you?" I nod and rake my nails down the side of his neck. "God, your body is a canvas I want to make mine and only mine."

I seize Brody's dirty talking mouth and come on his cock and balls like it's my right. I can hardly move but Brody doesn't waver. His breathing deepens and his thighs roll into mine. I nearly sing in pleasure, and it causes Brody to hold me closer.

"You were right," he grits out. I can't speak and he knows it. "You are my worst nightmare."

CHAPTER 5

Roxy

I CAN'T CONTROL MYSELF. I ALREADY WANT MORE. HE'S sticky from my orgasm, which also coats my inner thighs. Exquisite pleasure wracks through me, and I never want to come back down to earth.

"I wanna fuck you," I tell him. "Please."

Shit. I begged. I never beg.

Brody removes his fingers from both of my entrances, then grabs a hold of my hips and begins to thrust his cock between our bodies, making sure it strikes my clit with a force only a man would need to get off on. He uses me for his own pleasure as he rubs out his orgasm. I spread my hips wider, wanting to give him what he needs.

My heavy breasts are bouncing in his face. He grabs my nipple and gives it a little twist before he's back on his grind and I'm breathless with desire.

Something comes over me, and I whisper, "I want you to wreck my pussy tonight. Tear into me. Make it hurt. Show me how you would own my cunt if I let you." I gasp from the heightened sensations.

He releases a deep groan. "I already planned to."

I love it. I love that he said that.

My eyes roll shut as his do. He's lost to the feel-good pleasure taking over. The fire we're creating between our bodies is outrageous. I'm shocked by the things I'm saying to him. But in a way, I want them to be real. He makes me think for a split second they could be.

"Does it make you hard to know my orgasm is dripping down to your asshole right now?"

"Oh fuck," he yells. "Fuck."

I bite his neck and then run my tongue along it. He strains, causing a vein to pop up, and I lick it again.

"Show me how you'll ruin me for all other men."

"Rox," he says under his breath.

I pull his hair, and he groans, arching his back under me. There is nothing, and I mean nothing, sexier than a man in the heat of passion enjoying himself. And Brody is incredible. I pull his tongue into my mouth and suck on it as I ride us toward the wave. His erection twitches between us.

"Get up on your knees, now. I'm going to paint your body with my come."

I do as he demands.

Brody palms his cock. My gaze drops to the purple tip and I watch as he releases his load. Thick streams shoot in different directions, hitting my thighs and even the pouch of my belly. I love watching a man orgasm. It's a glorious thing to witness.

Brody swipes two fingers across my thigh and brings the fluid to my nipple. He paints over the glossy raspberry nub, then leans forward to lick it off. My lips part in surprise watching him lick his own pleasure. His hand finds my pussy and he rubs his semen on me. Our gazes are locked on one another. I'm mesmerized. It's dirty. It's wrong. We only just met.

I should tell him to stop, but I don't. I can't.

I move my hips and grind my pussy into his welcoming hand. Before I can stop it, a rush of euphoria bursts through me.

"Oh fuck! Brody." I rear my hips back, pulling away from his touch and instantly miss it. "I want to. I'm so close. God . . ." is all I can muster out. "I need . . ."

"You dirty little girl," he says, and I groan in response from the orgasm building between my hips. "You like seeing my cum on your cunt like that." I nod. It's erotic. "It got you horny again to see the filth on you. Ever watch a man's cum leak out of your pussy?"

Reaching down, I wrap my fingers around his cock and stroke it. I know there's a condom in my purse somewhere, but I can't stop right now. It's stupid and irresponsible, but I need him inside of me, and I need him now. The heat of the moment has never been this good.

"If your cum drips out of my pussy, you better lick it up and put it back in." His blue eyes light up with illicit thoughts. It sends chills down my spine.

"You filthy fucking slut," he says, and it both shocks and evokes me.

I squeeze my eyes shut, fighting my orgasm. He snickers under his breath and shifts, shoving the material at his hips to his thighs. I've never been called a slut before, but the way he says it has me over the edge. Somewhere in the back of my convoluted mind I know he doesn't mean it in a derogatory way. It's not something I would typically put up with. But Brody can call me anything he wants if he brings me pleasure this good.

"Only for you," I all but sing to him. "Brody, please," I beg, needing more.

"I got you."

Taking his open palm, he rubs my pussy in a fast circle. My hips move on their own account, and I let out a loud moan from the simple act of him letting me ride his hand without reserve. I pray no one can hear me outside these walls.

"You know you can't shove your pussy in my face like this and not expect me to taste you."

I glance down, frowning. I didn't realize he was level with my hips.

Without asking, Brody takes his thumbs and spreads

open my lips to reveal my reddened clit. His mouth is on it before I can blink, sucking me off while his tongue strokes down the seam to my entrance. My body tenses from the ridiculous pleasure wracking through me. Brody wraps his arms around my hips and holds me to him, making sure I can't move his mouth from my sex. I offer up my hips as much as I can at this angle.

"Oh, hell yes." I relish in his beautiful face, pulling on his hair again from the pleasure. "That's right, eat me." I buck and shove his face as hard as I can between my thighs. "Eat my pussy," I tell him again, shocked by my brazenness. His tongue is rapid and flat. He speeds up, then sucks me. He loves it as much as I do and motorboats me before sticking the tip of his tongue into my entrance. "Where have you been all my life?" I cry out. He abruptly pulls back and aligns the tip of his cock with my entrance.

"I'm about to wreck your pussy," he claims, then takes me by the hips and shoves me down on his cock.

We both yell out in unison. Tingles break out over my body, and I know he feels it too by his breathing and panting. My thighs convulse around his waist, my tender sex stretching to take his grith. I feel each centimeter of him I take in. My head rolls back from the unexpected rapture. Brody pushes me down further on his cock until I'm shaking from the intrusion, but he doesn't let me get acclimated to his length. He seizes my mouth and kisses me while thrusting his hips into mine, forcing me to accept him. His cock is huge and bare and feels too perfect inside my pussy, like it's where he belongs. it hurts. His width is making me burn and I clench. When I do, he shoves me down to take more of him. I begin rocking, knowing I'm about to get the best of both worlds.

"Still want me to eat it?" he asks, breaking the kiss.

"You will later," I say, looking into his eyes. I'm lost to him. "Keep your cock where it belongs."

His grin makes my heart flutter.

It doesn't take long before we're climbing the peak together. We fuck like banshees, the sex intense and filled with slamming hips and desperate cries. His cock pummels into me, and I meet him stroke for stroke. The chaise lounge we're on shifts under us and drags across the floor from the pounding we're giving each other. We just met and we can't get enough of each other.

"How the fuck do you move like that?" he asks as I hit the crest. I'm moving faster than him, my pussy walls stroking him raw. My ass bounces and his balls slap against me.

"I don't think," I tell him. "I just feel . . . And I take."

Brody shoves his cock so far into me that I still. The tip of his thick shaft twitches and I can feel it hit my cervix. A little squeak escapes me.

"Then I'm gonna take you too," he says, his voice low and dangerous. "I'm not gonna think. I'm just gonna fucking take you."

All I can say is, "Yes, please," and Brody goes to town.

My mind lets go, and he takes, giving me pleasure at the same time. Bliss climbing to the top, I start to shake. This doesn't feel like a normal orgasm threatening to spill. This one feels different, deeper, and I want it so bad I can taste it.

"Don't hold back, just come on my cock," Brody says, and I do.

Wrapping my arms around his shoulders, I find his lips and give him my orgasm. He helps get me there, and when I feel it burst from within me, I ride him to the ground and come harder than I ever have. I yell, not caring if anyone hears this time as I clench his cock with my pussy and milk him. Wetness is gushing out of me, so much so that I stop kissing him to look.

"Fuck, babe, are you squirting?" His eyes widen and his mound strains with a prominent vein where our bodies connect. It disappears under my pink flesh. "You're a squirter, aren't you? Shit, you are."

"I don't know. I've never done this before."

"Don't fuckin' stop," he tells me. "Keep doing it. I'm gonna spit in that pussy."

It sounds disgusting, but I can't wait. He takes me to the edge and wrings out every drop of my pleasure. I'm unable to speak. Brody is something out of a sex dream with the stamina of ten Viagras between his legs. I want to keep him forever.

"I'm coming, babe, I'm coming. Fuck, fuck, fuck." He moans and drives into me hard and passionately.

"You better fucking kiss me then or I jump off."

CHAPTER 6

Roxy

HIS MOUTH IS ON MINE BEFORE I CAN EVEN GET THE words out. Brody lets go and releases his pleasure, seeming to like that I ordered him to kiss me. If he didn't, then I don't think he would have listened, or made that guttural sound in his throat.

His cum shoots hot spurts into me, his shaft jerking as he pumps into me. I can feel it, and all it does is make me want to ride him more. We hold on to each other, kissing hard as our hips pound into one another, and we ride the wave of ecstasy we're fighting to stay on together. He rolls his hips under me and pushes deep. I undulate on him. It's pure bliss, and judging by his heavy panting, Brody feels good too. His warmth seeps out and coats my inner thighs. His hands are back on my butt cheeks, moving them around like he's juggling basketballs. We're sticky and sweating and our hips have slowed to a steady rhythm. The pungent, heady scent of sex fills the space between us. Our tongues slow but the fever between us doesn't. Brody is a lover who fights as he loves. His passion is unmatched.

He brushes the hair away from my face and I lean into his palm. He thumbs my bottom lip and pulls on it. I don't want to move. I'm completely spent and currently dying from the best orgasms of my life.

"You taste too good." Something about that makes me smile. "Like a drug. Too good to let go of after one taste."

"I don't want to get up," I tell him softly, wiggling my ass on him.

His cock is still hard in me. I rock on him, and he doesn't seem to mind. I like the soft, silky slow feel of his mound against my bare flesh kissing my clit. Any attention to that little bud will make me beg on my knees for more.

"You're mine tonight," he tells me, his voice low. "Come home with me."

My teeth dig into my bottom lip and I quickly nod. I *want* to be his. The corners of his lips curl in satisfaction. Shyness captures me and I glance away. His hips slowly drive into mine, taunting me with both his cock and deviant baby blues. I get lost in his gaze. I can tell Brody doesn't just like sex, he loves it. Like me. I think he gets high off it.

"I guess you'll be eating my cock for breakfast too, *Betty*."

My brows rise and before I can contain it, I start giggling. Brody leans forward and wraps his arms around me, joining me in the laughter.

"You think I'm kidding," he says, pressing his mouth to the curve of my neck. He exhales and I feel his heat curl around my throat. "I'm already fantasizing about you sitting on my face. I want your sweet thighs wrapped around my neck, suffocating me." His hands skim my hips seductively. "And your unholy pussy in my face." It's on the tip of my tongue to say something slick when he adds, "Why do you feel so fucking good. Damn." The words come from deep in his chest, and I feel them wrap around me. "I just wanna stay in this pussy and fuck you all night."

His proclamation makes me soar inside. He's as intoxicating as a bottle of tequila.

"Who's stopping you?" I ask coyly. "You wanna go hard all night? You're a party animal."

His tongue licks a hot trail over my collarbone. He smashes his face between my cleavage. "Till the sun rises."

"Obsessed with me already?"

His answer is to drag his tongue over my breast before he clamps down and bites me hard. His teeth dig, threatening to break the clump of skin he has in his mouth. I hiss and clench around him, my eyes rolling shut. His palm glides the arc of my neck. He threads his fingers through my hair, then drags my mouth to his. He kisses me deeply, savagely, and with a rawness I could easily get addicted to. It's like he knows how to make me want him.

"As much as I hate to see you get off my dick, get up, beautiful, and let's see the damage you did."

I take a deep breath, it's now or never. Brody loosens his hold around me as I stand and step to the side.

I don't move. I can't. I'm fixated watching him give his shaft one long, hard stroke before he wipes off the remnants on the side of the chair so casually. Lifting his hips, he takes his still hard dick and pushes it back into his pants. It looks uncomfortable bending it at the angle he does.

Brody stands and steps away. I hold my breath. If he were wearing lighter jeans, it would look like he urinated on himself. I turn to see the space we just occupied.

I palm my mouth and stifle back a laugh. It's so embarrassing it's almost comical. It looks like someone spilled a full drink.

Brody appears next to me and drops to one knee. I watch as he pushes my knees open and leans in to peer under my dress. I'm about to baulk at him when he takes the napkin in his hand and uses it to wipe my thighs clean. I don't move. I'm too stunned by this random act of kindness and remain quiet as he drags the tissue from my knee to the inside of my thigh until most of it is gone.

"Do I say thank you?"

His face softens and the smile he gives me is one I haven't seen yet. *It's really fucking cute.*

Brody wipes away any piece of evidence, then grabs the elastic around my waist from the remnants of my thong and rips it off. He hands it to me balled up, and I tuck it into my purse like it's a normal thing for us.

He throws the napkins away, then fills two shot glasses with Hennessey that he plucked from the mini bar. We don't say anything as we throw them back together, our eyes never leaving the other.

"Give me another," I tell him. And he does. He takes one too.

Brody takes my shot glass and places it on the counter next to his. "Turn around." Frowning, I do as he says, but I look over my shoulder to watch his gaze. His brows furrow before he reaches down to wipe a drop of cum from my thigh. He licks his finger clean and then says, "Let's go."

We head downstairs and take the exit through the back. I push open the door and see Estelle come off the wall immediately, a cigarette pressed to her lips. Her eyes light up when she sees me.

Estelle exhales a cloud of smoke, and says, "Hey, where've you been?"

"Getting fucked," Brody answers behind me.

Estelle's eyes shoot straight to Brody. Her brows rise, then she purses her lips and takes another puff while nodding her head in approval. Brody is glued to my backside with his hands on my hips. There's a possessiveness in his

49

touch that causes me to lean back into him and soak it up. He throws his arm over my shoulder and dangles his hand over my chest. Estelle notices and I roll my lips between my teeth and bite down. I'm ready for her to say something slick with that look in her eyes.

"I hope it was a top ten book worthy kinda fuck."

"The night is still young, and she's coming home with me."

I'm still feeling the tingle between my thighs. I lean back further and feel his hardness press into my ass. He nestles me deeper into him, making sure I feel it.

Estelle reaches out to shake his hand, but Brody refuses. "Nah, my hands were in every hole of hers I could fill. I'm Brody."

She giggles at my horrified look. If I didn't like his dick so much, I would tell him to fuck off. But that's not the case. Just thinking about what's hanging between his legs causes me to wiggle my hips into his.

"Did he make it to the gold-plated book of dick?"

"He's on his way," I say, taunting him.

Brody bobs his head, impressed. "You women never cease to amaze me."

"Not everyone can have the golden ticket," I tell him. "Gotta show me what you're working with first."

"Exactly why we're friends." Estelle jokes, then looks at me. "So, did you like the show?" Her eyes are hopeful.

"Surprisingly I did." I pause and frown. "Wait. How did you end up out here?"

"You don't even want to know." Her eyes glitter under the lights and a smirk paints her face. I feel her excitement and need to know more.

"Tell me," I demand, trying not to laugh. "Tell me what you did."

Flicking the butt of her cigarette to the ground, she steps on it with a twist. She exhales and opens her mouth to speak when a blacked-out truck with a muffler that sounds like it's full of rust pulls to a stop about thirty feet from us.

I recognize the driver's face as one of the guys singing on stage. I'm just trying to remember which part of the band the guy is in. Their eyes meet and the only sounds are the horns in the distance. I feel like he may be the reason why she's been trapped out here.

Estelle hesitates, then turns to look at me. She blinks and I'm about to shove her in his direction because I'm pretty sure that's the lead singer.

"We good?" she asks, eyes full of hope. I grab her face and smack a loud kiss to her cheek. She smiles back at me before skipping off.

What the guys don't know is that Estelle and I have this pact to make sure we are truly okay to part ways alone. We don't want to end up in a ditch somewhere. It's one reason why we never bring men back to our house and always track the other's location.

Estelle walks around the beater of a truck and climbs in, slamming the door. It sounds like it's going to fall off. They take off and Brody spins me around, pushing me up against the brick wall before I can even blink. A breath lodges in my throat as his hand travels toward my pelvis. I don't know why I'm responding to him the way I am, like I'm aching for him, but I don't question it.

My hips rear forward in response, meeting his erection. His hand cups my pussy over my dress. I wish he'd move the damn material. Brody growls in my ear, and by God do I melt at the sound of it. He moves into me so seductively that for a moment I forget where I am.

"Tell me one more time you're mine tonight."

My lips part and I tell him with conviction, "I'm yours tonight."

CHAPTER 7

Brody

WHILE ROXY WAS TALKING TO HER GIRLFRIEND, I had my driver on standby and shot him a quick text to get his ass ready to ride around the back and grab us.

I need to get this woman alone immediately.

Naked and under me.

Or over me.

I bet she's the type to want to be in charge, and sometimes I like that. There's nothing sexier than watching a woman who feels comfortable with herself when she's naked.

But not tonight.

Not after what she just did in the VIP room. I need to have my way with her first with the way she just orgasmed all over my cock. Roxy was free, her body was pliant, and fuck me, she was juicy as hell. Anywhere I grabbed her body made my dick ache to grip her harder. And when I did, her pussy fucking contracted around me. She liked it when I applied pressure.

I love a woman I can hold on to. One who can take a pounding and not cry. I want to feel like I'm going to break her, not actually worry that I will.

I suck in a breath as my cock strains against my damp jeans. A squirter. A fucking squirter, and she didn't know.

I'm going to make her do it again. I've never had a woman do that before and it almost made me want to make her mine for a little while. I don't date though. Like Roxanne said, too many pussies to taste test to settle on one. I like that all we have is tonight.

I can't fucking wait to be deep inside her pussy again. She's pushing against me now, trying to entice me, but what she doesn't know is that she's already got me for the night. Fuck a condom tonight. There's no point after we already had sex without it. Not after knowing how she feels bare. She dripped like honey for me.

Roxanne responded differently. She responded the way a woman should, one who was on the edge of pure bliss.

She wasn't faking it either, and it triggered something inside me to watch her unfold. She was magnificent. She let go the way a lioness would roar and the cry was felt around the forest. I was enthralled. She was all I could focus on. All I could hear. All I wanted.

She wants me to call her Roxy, but Roxanne is too much of a woman for that. Roxy is a side chick you ride hard and put away wet, and when you run into her two months from now, you can't remember where you've seen her.

I want to dig into Roxanne and unleash myself on her. I want to know what ticks her off and what makes her feel good, so when we have sex, she can't tell if we're fucking or making love. A little bit of both makes the pleasure intensify, and I'm all about making my body feel good, all day every day. Either it comes from a warm pussy, or a few pills and a bottle of Jack, I'm going to get off.

It's rare I fuck without protection. Or in a club. I'm a little surprised I let it happen, but I'm tested every six months, so I know I'm clean. Plus, I can't remember the last time I slipped. This city is filthy and most of the residents are looking for a handout or sleeping their way up the chain. I may be addicted to sex, but I'm not usually careless about it.

Roxanne screams bougee posh princess. They're usually the ultra-prude types who say they want a bad boy but can't handle the package.

Which means they wouldn't dare cross contaminate. Those girls suck dick with a condom on.

No-fucking-thanks.

Roxanne is a princess, no doubt, probably some socialite who comes from money. But she's not a prude, and she likes to get dirty.

So I need to know if she's clean because I'm about to have her leaking from every angle.

The second Roxanne said goodbye to Estelle, I made my move. She's got a pussy I want to escape in. I hate to be all John Mayer, but I get it now when he said "your body is a wonderland."

"I didn't use a rubber. I need to know—"

"I'm clean," she says quickly. Her back straightens. "I'm, um, clean. For what it's worth, I don't usually do that." Her back straightens further. "I'm on birth control too."

It's on the tip of my tongue to ask her if she's ever felt the lust of a cock without a barrier between her juicy thighs before. I don't though. It doesn't really matter in the end. All that matters is now.

I hear the tires of a large car pull up the alleyway and know it's my driver. He's always on point. A quick glance over my shoulder confirms it.

"Ready to get the hell out of here?"

The door is opened for us, and we climb in. She looks around, her hazel eyes taking in the custom-built Mercedes SUV. The second row and the third row face each other, and there's a foldable table for the center that's stowed away. The car is equipped with a mini bar and a Bose stereo system, and a divider that encases us in complete privacy.

"Not bad, playboy. Where are you taking me?" she asks, reaching for the crystal decanter and two glasses.

Roxanne pops the top and brings it to her nose, inhaling. I have no idea what's in there and she doesn't seem to care either. My head tilts to the side, pleased that she didn't look at me and see dollar signs. Because I don't have them. My paintings have made me a pretty penny, but it's not consistent. And not for lack of trying. Nude paintings of women are in popular demand. However, finding nude models that I connect with doesn't come easy. I can't just paint anyone. And I won't.

Roxanne though? I'd create a series with her body.

I didn't just see a woman I wanted to sink myself into for a couple of hours when I looked at her. A mirage had appeared before me, a succession of images of only her. Every time I blinked a new one emerged.

My legs carried me before I knew what I was doing. I was going to ask her for her number until I got closer and felt *her*. Like she was some sort of a goddess or some shit. I've never had that happen before.

Shades of color surrounded her in a wave of heat I was drawn to unlike I'd ever seen, and not because of the toxic shit I'd fed my veins right before. I'm always fucked up on something, but I never hallucinate. I like enough to take the edge off and keep me riding smooth.

My thoughts shift to the harmony we created when we touched. She was overflowing with a glitter of colors, and that stirred the artist lying dormant in me.

"Hey, playboy?" she says softly, her voice bringing me back to reality. "Where'd you go?"

Blinking, I look straight at her. "I was admiring your beauty." It sounds cheesy, but it's the truth. Roxanne is gorgeous in ways Hollywood typically deems unacceptable, and that's what I like about her.

Her chin dips to her chest like she's suddenly shy and doesn't know she's pretty. That's blasphemy. I'm not here to stroke a woman's ego, so I answer her previous question about where we're heading.

"Santa Monica."

"Love it there. I don't live too far."

Noted.

She passes one glass to me and pours out more than a shot, then gives one to herself. "I have a couple of friends in the area. Are you on the beach?"

"Close to it."

"Close enough to walk?"

"Enough with the small talk," I tell her, setting my glass down in the built-in cup holder. "Come here with your sexy ass."

She chuckles, smiling behind her glass. I take it from her and put it in the holder next to mine, then I pat my lap, needing her on me. I want to taste her before I taste the liquor that will kill her sweetness.

Her gaze drops to where my hand is. She watches as I get adjusted. My thighs spread and my hips heave, the bulge in my pants growing. If she looks closely enough, she can see the outline of the tip of my cock. I run my thumb over it and watch her eyes narrow. A low groan rumbles in my chest. Roxanne has the ability to turn me into an animal with the fucking sounds I'm making.

Sue me for getting off on a beautiful woman watching me touch my cock.

Music streams through the speakers and the base hits low. My blacked-out SUV is soundproof. So when J. Cole comes on, it sets the scene, the females want to dance and grind. It does the trick, and with a glint in her eyes, she makes her way to me.

I can't help myself and automatically slide my hands under her dress to reach for the sugarplums she calls an ass. It was the first thing I thought of when I saw her dancing— two sugarplum ass cheeks I wanted to take a bite out of.

I massage the back of her thighs to let her know I want her to feel good and relax on me. My palms roam up her thighs to the crease of her hips and dig in. She slow dances on me, pushing her huge tits in my face that are barely contained by her dress. The touch of supple, baby soft skin meets my lips. She cups the back of my head and I inhale her essence. My hands are all over her like I'm a fucking addict and can't stop.

She's like touching velvet. Roxanne curves into my body like she's fucking designed to.

A need ignites inside of me, a burn I'm not familiar with. I typically only get like this when I'm painting.

"Play a game with me," Roxanne says close to my ear, her voice husky.

"Yeah? What kind of game is that?"

"Promise me you'll say yes first."

She's too fucking cute. I was already going to.

Roxanne pulls back to meet my gaze and begins to move seductively. She wants my dick, and she wants it bad.

"Say it first," she demands.

The smile in her eyes entices me. If she wants to play, I can to.

"If I make you a deal blindly, then you gotta make one for me, babe."

I don't know why the fuck I keep calling her babe. It just slips out when she demands shit I give no one but want to give to her.

"Deal," she says quickly, then pulls my mouth to hers and kisses me.

I'm pretty much a goner at this point until we pull into my driveway.

One, I wasn't expecting her to know the fucking song and hit every beat with her goddamn ass. Her bouncing on me is basically jerking me off.

And two, I can tell Roxanne is reckless, irresponsible, and wild in the time I've met her. And that gets my nuts off more than anything.

She's uninhibited.

Like me.

I want to know what's in her wildest dreams.

CHAPTER 8

Brody

THIS IS WHAT I GET FOR THINKING WITH MY DICK.
Luckily the ride back to the house isn't long.
It's just enough time to make this dumb fucking deal with her and want to kill myself for it.

I don't know how my cock is going to last.

"On the count of three," she says, handing me mine. "And you better take it all."

The strap of her dress slips off her creamy shoulder. She leaves it. I can tell she's got a bad streak. She's chasing a high, but she doesn't want to do it alone. Fighting for euphoria is only as good as the person you're getting it with.

Roxanne has no idea just how sexy she is. I can't take my eyes off her.

"Tell me how you expect this to work," I say. This deal just isn't processing in my head.

I put our glasses away and cup her ass in my lap to listen. I'm all ears.

Hazel eyes peer into mine. "Simple. Just make out with me. No penetration." She pauses and holds up her index finger. "Of any sorts." My brows rise. "No blow jobs, and you can't have your tongue in any part of me but my mouth." My eyes widen. This woman is fucking crazy. "And no orgasms," she says, confirming my worst nightmare. "Not until we get to your place."

"What? No. Why?" It's all I can say. The idea is dumb. "Why? Why would you want to suffer like that?"

"Don't get greedy. Pleasure comes to those who wait. When you do come for me, you're going to sing my name up to the stars.

When I come for her? This woman makes me want to choke her and fuck her at the same time. She doesn't tell me when I come.

But fuck, it does things to my cock when she talks like that.

"You think you got this all figured out."

Either she's got a good pair of bedroom eyes, or this

is all Roxanne. She whispers near my ear, "That's when the real fucking starts. The kind that blows your mind."

A low laugh escapes me. She has no idea who she's playing with.

"You're going to regret this. Game on, baby."

Her teeth dig into her bottom lip. Her lashes flutter. "I hope so."

Unable to hold back, I need her lips on mine. I like this girl too much. She feeds a darker part of me I've long suppressed.

Something tells me I just met my match.

"I'll play your game, but you have to do it my way."

Her subtle nod is my green light.

I gaze above her head to the decanter she left uncorked. She feels good in my arms, so I reach for it with the other hand and bring the bottle to my lips. I peer down at her as I take a swig, then offer it to her. She opens and I hold the bottle to her mouth and watch as she takes a swallow without cringing. A drop falls from the corner of her mouth. Without thinking, I lean in and kiss her while licking it away.

Roxanne's exquisite. Fuck. She's almost too perfect and she responds better than I could have asked for. Her cool tongue delves around mine as her hand comes up to cup the back of my head, the other reaches for my cock. She's smooth as melting ice. I don't do things half-assed, and I grab her anywhere I can, shoving my tongue in her mouth to get this show going. I kiss the fuck out of her and hold her close. I don't stop. If this is what she wants, then I'll give it to her.

By the time we get to my place, I all but throw her out of the door the second my driver opens it. She stumbles near the bushes, drunk, but holds herself together. Unlike me.

The pressure between my hips is raging. I'm so into her and can't form proper thoughts to think straight. My dick hurts from the orgasm she wouldn't let me have and it makes it all that much better. I don't think I'm going to make it two steps in the house with how blue my balls are.

Taking her hand in mine, I lead her to the tall black front doors and press the code into the lock box. The door opens and I pull her inside with me. Roxanne drops her purse on the floor, then tackles me. Most women I bring back to the house want to ooh and ahh first. Not this one.

She just wants my dick.

Roxanne is aggressive, and I know it's because of her stupid game. She shoves me against the wall and rips off my shirt, tugging it over my head and throwing it behind her. She reaches for my jeans but stalls. I kick off my shoes.

A burn crawls up my chest as she takes in the colorful art that stains my skin. The artist in me wants to see what she's made of inside.

"Do . . ." She swallows. "Do you live alone?"

The question baits me. "No. Why?"

"Anyone else here?"

She hasn't torn her eyes off me. It's so fucking stimulating that I pause to think about her question. I can't think straight. If the guys were home, they'd be in the billiards room where we shoot the shit, breaking each other's balls. While some of the lights were left on, their voices would carry if they were here.

Roxanne brings her hands up to touch the thin needle lines. She traces them delicately like she's trying to figure out where they lead. I grab her wrist to stop her. Her eyes snap to mine. Now that I can finally see them in the light, they're entwined with shades of topaz and emerald.

My eyes roam hers. I don't know why I'm so into this one tonight, but my life has given me something to look forward to. Eyes are the gates to the soul, and hers are begging me to bust the motherfucking doors down.

"No one is here but us."

She cups my jaw and pulls me in for a kiss that is anything but lackluster. She's a goddamn fire starter.

I could barely get the words out before her dress hits the floor and she drops to her knees. My brows bunch as I watch Roxanne remove my jeans until I'm thwarted by the sight of her at this angle. She's got two little dimples at the small of her back and a heart-shaped ass that I want to rub down with honey. Her knees are spread open, her back bowed. I take in the view and wonder if she was sent here to kill me with how her ass splits down her milky cheeks that leads to a place I can't see. Like she's hiding the goodies to taunt me.

"Get up here," I tell her.

She made me wait in the car, and now I'm fired up. I need her, now.

"Hang on," she says, then shocks me. Roxanne wraps her hand around my cock and takes me into her mouth.

My head flies back and slams into the wall. I wasn't expecting that. She sucks me hard the second her lips touch my cock, and she doesn't stop. Her mouth has a vice grip as she bobs up and down. I can't remember a time I've been sucked so good. My hand finds the back of her head and I thread my fingers through her hair, fisting it. Her tongue is working my shaft and building me up much faster than I'm ready for.

"Rox," I say, and I don't even sound like myself. Rox? Now I'm on a nickname basis with her. This is what good head does to you. "Rox, wait."

I try to pull her back, but she just goes harder and sucks me deeper. My chest rises and falls fast. I need to stop her because I want to fuck her, but I'm lost to the heat of her mouth and her wicked tongue. She makes me feel too good.

"Stop sucking my dick and get up here."

I can't believe I just said those words. I've never told a woman to stop sucking me before, but then I've never met anyone like Roxy.

Roxanne shakes her head and continues. When she

takes my free hand and guides it to the back of her head where my other hand is, my hips take on their own pulse. She's asking me to fuck her mouth.

No, she's begging me to.

"You pull away now or I'm coming in your mouth." She shakes her head in response, unable to speak. "I'm warning you."

"I'm thirsty," she says around my cock, and I almost laugh.

"It's a big one," I warn her.

"I'm parched," she says, and this time I do laugh. I like this girl.

I'm rolling into the oblivion too fast. She takes me too deep and taunts me just right. My orgasm crawls down my spine and attacks me before I know it. My hips surge, my balls tighten. Roxanne holds me hostage with her mouth as my breathing becomes erratic, and before I know it, I'm coming hard. Roxanne nudges her knees closer to drink me down. She doesn't stop. She keeps the same pace and same friction, she just blows me harder, better. I don't hold back and release my pent-up orgasm into her relentless mouth. She drinks it down like she's draining me dry.

"Fuck me," I whisper, coming down from the most incredible feeling. I'm going to have dreams of her tongue now after what she just did.

"That's the plan," she says, her voice raspy. I glance down and see the clear line of fluid drip from her lips to the tip of my still hard cock. This woman's got me tingling from head to toe right now.

She stands in front of me and uses the back of her hand to wipe off the excess. I watch, enthralled. There's not a drop of cum left inside me, but that won't keep me down for long. Not when there's a woman like Roxanne in front of me.

"Give me those lips," I demand.

CHAPTER 9

Brody

I REACH OUT AND YANK HER MOUTH TO MINE.

We kiss in a frenzy, stepping away from the wall and stumbling to the next. I love a good fight for sex, and she's just as starved for it as I am. The buildup, the anticipation, to know that eventually I'm going to make my way inside of her makes me unstoppable.

I bump into a small accent table and tip over some knickknacks the interior designer insisted we have. They lay forgotten in a heap as we move toward the living room.

"Where's your bed?" she mumbles against my lips. She nips me.

"Who needs a bed when you have a wall?" I say, then push her against the first one I see. I reach down and cup the back of her thighs to lift her up. Her legs wrap around my hips and I nestle closer to her, needing to feel the heat of her against me. Her wet pussy rubs my pelvis. I can't wait to be inside of her again.

"We can fuck right here," I say against her mouth, but she puts a hand on my chest and pulls back.

"Put me down."

I frown, but I don't put her down. "Why?"

She blinks a few times and unlocks her ankles, then tries to shimmy her way out of my arms.

Fuck that.

I adjust her and hold her tighter. "Tell me why."

"Just put me down and bend me over a couch." My frown deepens as I try to figure out where I went wrong. It was going so smooth. "It's easier that way."

I'm lost here. "Easier for who? You? Am I hurting you?"

She blinks like a deer in headlights, as if it's obvious. I wait for an answer, and when she doesn't give it, I lean in to bite her bottom lip. I'd never force myself on a woman, but Roxanne is different. I can sense it in my chest. She wanted this. Something changed. I need to know what went wrong.

"Rox. What's going on in your head? What severed the connection?"

"It would be easier for both of us if I just bend over for you. You don't have to hold me up."

Looking into her eyes, I see what she's hiding. Her chest lifts into mine, a flush of red colors her cleavage. She still wants me, I can see it in the way she looks at me, but it's her hesitation that stalls my next move.

Her tongue darts out to wet her lips. Roxanne withers against me and lets out a little grunt under her breath. She's frustrated. I can taste it. This gorgeous girl thinks she's too heavy for me to lift and it's probably why she wants me to put her down. It's no wonder why she made that comment about cellulite earlier.

Unless she doesn't like this position? The pounding is harsher at this angle and not everyone I've found likes it.

I test out the theory.

"Is it the position? Don't like the wall? Hard for you to get off? Can't come?"

She frowns. Maybe I'm way off myself. She stares at me like I'm an imbecile, and it's making me uncomfortable. I'm usually a pretty good judge of character.

"I make sure I get mine," she says with a straight face that causes a pinch in my heart.

I like this girl.

"Then what the fuck is it?"

She rolls her eyes to the side, exasperated. "I slipped once, okay." I shake my head, not following. "Like I fell through," she says, but I still don't get it. She blinks a few times and I feel like she wants me to read her mind.

"Like you slipped off a dick?" My words come out in a fit of laughter. I didn't mean to laugh, but the thought makes me cackle. "Was he a pencil dick?" I ask, curious how the hell you slip off a cock now.

"No, you brainiac." Roxanne is casual as she tosses the sarcasm at me. Like she's comfortable, and it does something funny to me. "He couldn't hold my ass up! His arms gave out. I folded like a sofa bed and slipped between his legs. I hit the marble floor and fractured my damn tailbone."

I can't believe my ears right now. I almost wonder if she's making this up. "His arms gave out?"

"I kneed myself in the nose."

She stares at me with a serious face while I fight off another round of laughter threatening to burst from me. The light in her eyes is dimming. I don't want Roxanne to think I'm laughing at her, because I'm not, but this is some funny shit if I ever heard it.

"Little boys always chewing off more than they can eat," I say, leaning into the curve of her neck. "I'm not one of them."

I don't hold back and bite down on the muscle along her shoulder. She tenses and I clamp down harder, forcing her to lock her ankles around my waist. Her back arches as she hisses. Her nails dig into my arm and score the skin. She grunts, holding back the pain, and all it does is rev me up.

"He make your dick book?"

"My what?" She pants, lost. Her head falls back, and her eyes roll shut.

"The book of gold dicks."

Her raspy giggle produces a grin from me. "You can't fucking be serious," Roxanne says. Her airy laugh makes me fall into her and drop a kiss to her cheek. "That's a negative, ghost rider," she adds.

There's a lightheartedness in the air that surrounds her. It invades my senses and draws me close. For the first time in weeks, I don't feel the underlying sense of doom in my chest. Her mouthy smile, the unapologetic tone of her sassy words, the way her voice crackles as she laughs, it's the making of a beautiful woman who glows from the inside out.

"Rox?" I say.

I get one taste of her pussy and now I'm calling her names like she's my lover or some shit. I shake my head and drop the thought for now.

"Hmm?"

"Do me a favor and grab my dick for me."

Her eyes snap to mine and she waits for further instructions. When she palms my length, I get lost in the sight of her pink pussy and hard clit spread out for me. I plan to make her come on my tongue later.

Roxanne gives me a good, long stroke. I hoist her up with ease and position her above my straining cock. I widen my stance to make sure she isn't going anywhere. I do it for her peace of mind, even though I know I won't drop her. She watches as I insert the tip of my mushroom head into her entrance. Her pussy lips flare like a blooming flower reaching for the sun.

"Look at me." Her eyes lift to mine. "I'm not going to drop you. Let the thought go now. The only thing I want you thinking about is how it feels when I'm inside of you. Nothing else. Got it?" She nods furiously.

Then I take her all the way to the hilt in one stroke. Roxanne yells out and my cock jerks inside of her at the sound. She feels good. She feels like home.

"Make all the noise you want. We're all alone."

And boy does she ever. She releases a sigh that sounds like she's singing. I slide in and out of her at a steady pace, making sure I buck my hips to stroke her clit at the same time. The impact makes her breathless, so I do it again. Her body quivers and I revel in it knowing that she feels good. Her ankles lock behind my back as her large breasts bounce into my chin. It makes me want to reach out with my teeth and bite her nipple.

"Tell me what you want."

Giving her what she wants gives me what I want. We both win.

"For you not to drop me."

Her winded words don't escape me. I don't know whether to laugh or shake my head. I'm not going to drop her, but I see her mind is still elsewhere, so I make a quick move.

Roxanne needs to feel like she's in control after what happened. I mean, there's no way she's slipping between my legs. She won't fit. Her hips are too wide to get past my thighs because I don't just work out my arms at the gym. She isn't going anywhere.

I carry her ass to the billiards room that we use for various things. Pool equipment is propped up haphazardly along the custom shelves. The glass blown fishhook knobs I designed are placed sporadically and hold various things. There's an old dart board, but all the darts are missing.

"What're you doing?" Roxy asks, and wraps her arms around my neck. Her tits press into my chest and my dick aches at the touch of her hot flesh.

I don't have time to explain myself, so I show her.

Her legs are squeezing me as I walk across the room to the pull-up bar. I step under and cage us in, betting that no one has ever carried her anywhere.

"Grab the bar and hold on," I tell her, then jostle her in my arms to reposition us. "Loosen your damn legs, Rox."

She does as I say and holds the bar with a look of confusion that I find cute. I squat a little to grab my dick and slide it back into her pussy. She gasps and I feel it in my throat.

"Situate yourself on my cock and hold on to the bar."

She stays quiet and does just that. She contracts around me, milking my cock. Her gaze turns eager. Roxanne bites the side of her mouth and rolls her hips into mine. She bears down, dragging her cunt over my flesh as much as she can with my cock inside of her. An illicit moan leaves her mouth. It's incredibly seductive and brings out this ravenous craving in me because she does it all while looking me in the eye.

She puts a show on for me.

My palm grazes her plump ass cheek, loving the way she feels in my hands. Once she's in place, I step closer to her until her back is completely against the wall and she can't move. One of her hands is firmly wrapped around the workout bar, but I pay it no attention. It's not important.

Our eyes meet and we take a moment. My bare cock is soaked in her warmth. We're closer than we've ever been, and there's something utterly imitate about it. We're strangers, but the way she's looking at me, like she's putting her trust in me right now, makes me want to honor what she's not saying.

"Better?"

She nods and my hips surge forward, deeper, harder. Her eyes don't leave mine. I'm tapping her ass and stroking her clit as I hit her cervix. I want to blow her mind with how she's looking into my eyes, and what better way to do it than give her the sex I know she secretly desires.

"Harder. I want it harder," she tells me. My eyes widen and excitement fuels me until she says, "I just don't know what to do with my legs."

I don't stop pumping into her. Roxanne is tall, close to my height, and I'm over six foot. If she lets go, her legs dangle to the floor.

The skin of my balls slaps into her ass. Her pussy contracts around my cock and my stomach dips. She's soaking wet and it's trickling down my thigh. I plunge inside her and bring her hips down as she meets me stroke for stroke.

She doesn't just hang around for me to do the job. Roxanne works for her pleasure.

But I can't help but notice her legs and how they're falling to the side now. This girl messes with my head.

Adjusting my stance, I grab her ankle and place her foot on my backside. Deadlifts at the gym all day. It'll get you both an ass and muscle to fuck a woman against a wall. Her knee comes up and the angle deepens. Roxanne cries out and my cock jerks.

She sounds like an angel in need.

"I have never . . ." She pauses, unable to get the rest of her words out as I continue to surge into her. "Ahh, Brody."

"Never what?"

She shakes her head. "F-felt so high from sex. You hit all the right places. I might actually have you for breakfast."

I hold her close and step away from the wall, then carry her to the pool table in the center of the room. I settle her down and then climb on top until she leans back. She stares up at me with glossy eyes and flushed cheeks. Her messy hair is a knot of curls.

I hover above her and say, "I'm not done with you." Then I reach between us to guide my cock back inside of her.

CHAPTER 10

Brody

I'M NOT SURE WHAT'S GOTTEN INTO ME BUT SHE'S MAK-
ing me crave sex like I'm some sort of addict when I'm
really not. Yeah, I have a healthy sex life and get relief
when I want, but this isn't just sex. And it isn't the orgasm
that turns me into a lover either. I feel like she's branded me.

I look into her hazel eyes and notice the color has mor-
phed into a lighter shade. I frown, wondering if it's the great
sex that did it.

"Got something to prove, playboy?" Her smile is more
of a taunt. "You take an erection pill?"

"A weaker man would be insulted. No, babe. This is all me and you."

The corners of her lips curve just slightly. She doesn't know I caught it.

I kiss her slow and fierce. I'm not pumping into her like an animal this time. She goes with the flow, and when she releases a moan, I know I'm doing something right. I cage her in with my elbows and lay on top of her gently, eager to feel her skin to skin.

Roxanne kneads me, pulls on the skin on my back and takes what she wants when heightened pleasure consumes her. Her hands reach down and cup my ass cheeks. I kiss her neck and pull her into me, making sure to not leave a hickey. She pumps me into her, hooks her leg around the back of mine, and uses my body for her own pleasure.

It makes me feel like a fucking king.

She makes me crazy.

Her little whimpers blend into her hisses and I kind of want to make her do them again.

"Rox?"

She giggles, and even her giggle is sexy.

What the hell is wrong with me saying cute again?

"Yeah?" Her voice is like a groggy Sunday morning.

"You good?"

I'm not sure what I'm asking her. I guess if what we did on the wall was better for her this time. I mean, I know it was. All signs point to yes. I hope that I erased the memory of her being too much of a woman and showed her that she's perfect the way she is.

"Oh, I'm good, playboy. I feel like I'm delirious." She giggles again and my balls tighten up. "Are you good? Because I heard you call me babe . . . baby . . . and now Rox."

Her cheesy smile makes the blood in my cheeks rise.

I'd rather not answer, so I snag her lips again, rocking against her hips. She twists her legs with mine, her fingers twirl in my hair, and I sink into her soft body. Roxanne is like being wrapped in cashmere under a golden sunset.

Who knew sex could be so . . . intimate?

It doesn't take long for the pleasure to rise between us before we're panting into one another, trying to catch our breaths. I can sense her impending orgasm climbing by the way she clenches around my dick. The fact that I have another nut threatening to explode from my balls shocks the shit out of me. I couldn't get a boner this fast, even in high school. No wonder she thinks I'm on Viagra.

We're already ascending the hike together when a thought comes to mind. It makes the blood in my cock thicken. While I wouldn't ask just anyone to try this, I feel like Roxanne would be more open to it.

"Want to kiss the stars tonight?" I ask near her ear.

"With you?"

I pull back and glare at her. "Yeah, me. Who else?"

"I don't know, the guy next door?"

She causes another grin to spread across my face. I know she's messing with me because she's still fucking me into her. She's unabashed when it comes to sex. Makes me think she likes it as much as I do.

"Try something with me," I say.

Pulling my erection out, I stop to take in her body laid out before me, bare, flushed from sex, and glowing like a stolen gem. I reach out with two fingers and gently graze her spread lips. I press them inside her entrance, then pull back to suck on them. Roxanne squeezes her thighs closed, watching me with heavy lids.

She moans. "Tell me what you want."

"I want to suffocate between your thighs, and right before you come, you're going to get on your knees right here on this pool table so I can come inside the only hole I haven't filled yet."

Her eyes widen. She hesitates, but I know if she just lets me try it will be everything she never even dreamed of feeling.

Roxanne's knees spread and I don't give her any chance to renege. I give my cock one more good stroke before I'm diving between her legs to get a taste.

"Fuck, Brody. Fuck."

She draws the words out as her back bows in pleasure. I hold her thighs to my head and flick her clit as she shamelessly uses my face to get off. My dick is aching as I dry rub the itchy ass fabric on the pool table while I eat her out. It's erotic as hell to me how she's so open.

"Is there anything you're not good at?" She jokes. "Goddamn, Brody. You're so wicked with that tongue." Her hips twist off the table and her thighs trap me. "It's almost as if you like it," she says, dragging the heel of her foot down the pool table.

I pop my head up from between her thighs and get a look of her glorious breasts. For a split moment I'm anxious to feel them in my hands. I was so focused on her pussy that I forgot anything else. I attempt to say something when she looks me in the eye and I get a better idea. I lean up on my elbows and spread open her swollen lips. They're puffy, filled with desire and aching for release.

I stick my tongue out and keep eye contact with her as I disappear between her legs. She can't see when I reach out with the tip of my tongue and tickle her puckered little hole. If she couldn't find a man to treat her right and use her like a rag doll against something as simple as a wall, then she damn sure hasn't been fucked the right way at all. I've been around the Hollywood scene enough to know what women fantasize about when they think no one is listening.

I knew what I was getting into with one look at her body, and I couldn't fucking wait. She's a total what you see is what you get package, and shit like that makes my balls tighten up. A confident girl in the sheets makes for a stunning girl on the streets.

My tongue is flat as I drag a slow wet trail up her pussy. The artist in me deeply appreciates the female body and all its wonders. They're much more complex creatures to figure out.

She squeezes my head with her thighs and I struggle

to lick her. She knows it and uses me to grind down on. Roxanne bears down hard, my nose getting lost between her folds. She's dripping wet all over my face and into my beard.

"Brody! Oh, I'm close."

I pull away and tug her up. She moves swiftly and sits on her knees in front of me, giving me her back.

She turns her head to peer over her shoulder, her ashy blond hair falling down her back. "Do I need to assume the position and get on all fours?" she asks.

And when she does, I use my middle finger to press on her puckered hole. She tenses when she finally understands that I want her ass.

"Bear down," I whisper. "I won't hurt you."

Surprisingly, she does. "I've only tried it once."

"And?" I ask.

She shrugs as if we're talking about the weather. "Wasn't anything to phone home about."

"You said tried. So you didn't actually do anal?"

She shakes her head. Leaning forward, I drop a kiss to her shoulder and she smiles back at me. Roxanne is an anal virgin.

I'm in heaven.

"Did it hurt?" I ask, probing the hole again with my finger. "Bear down again and relax."

"All I could focus on was the pain and how his tiny dick was able to cause so much of it."

A chuckle erupts from me. Roxanne keeps me entertained in ways I didn't know were possible.

"Did he use lube?"

"Actual lube? No."

I shake my head in disbelief. Rookie move. "Don't tell me he used his spit. This better not be the same guy who you slipped off of."

"Two different guys." Her raspy voice is sexy.

Now that I know where I'm at with Roxanne, for her to get off on anal sex, I need to do it the right way for the both of us. Unfortunately, what I need is down the hall in my room. Not only is she going to need lube, but I am too.

"Stay right here and don't move. I need to grab something."

She peers her doe eyes over her shoulder and pouts. "You're gonna leave me alone in this big ol' house? Whatever shall I do?" she says in a sugary, soft southern style voice.

Roxanne's a classic beauty. A contemporary Marylin Monroe. The facets she's shown me already in this short amount of time is enough to make me delve deeper.

Roxanne is a muse.

She's my muse.

"I want you to touch yourself until I get back. I'll be quick."

She nods and then reaches between her legs to play with her pussy while she keeps her gaze on me. Her mouth falls open and I glance down. Roxanne knows I'm watching her and rubs herself shamelessly on her hand, her glorious ass open and waiting for me. I can't help myself and take her cheeks into my hands and spread them further. She does a slow, dry hump and tips her hips back for me. My lips part and my cock is straining at the sight.

"Better hurry back. I can easily make myself go like this." She taunts me, and I fucking run.

I'm back in a matter of seconds, less than thirty, and I nearly trip over the side table next to the couch when I see Roxanne.

My mind was spinning with ideas as I sprinted to my room and grabbed a new bottle of lube and sash. I like an assortment of toys to use on myself and other lovers, but I don't share any that I would need to insert. For many reasons.

Only, when I return, Roxanne stuns me. My gaze immediately goes to the drop of liquid distending from her pussy to the table.

She's bent over with her face to the table and her ass in the air, her heavy cheeks spread wide for my viewing pleasure.

I swallow thickly. I think I'm gonna marry this girl.

CHAPTER 11

Brody

" I HAD TO STOP TOUCHING MYSELF OR ELSE I WAS going to come without you. So to keep my hands busy from that happening, I thought you might like this instead."

There's a knot in my throat now. Yeah, I'm gonna have to lock this girl down somehow.

I close the distance between us, our gaze never wavering from the other's. I've never had sex on a pool table, let alone one I share with my roommates, but I guess there's a first time for everything.

Roxanne stares back at me, the glossy look no longer present in her eyes. I imagine the liquor has left her body the way it has for me. I love a good drunk fuck, but nothing is going to compare to what comes next.

Climbing up, I sit behind her raised hips and look at her two holes I'm going to fucking devour tonight. She hasn't moved and something about that pleases me immensely.

Her hole is tight, too puckered up for my cock, but I'm not worried about that. I'm going to make her feel so good, she's not going to realize how big my dick is until after we're done.

"You were right," I tell her, thinking back to something I remember she said earlier.

"About what?"

"You're my worst nightmare because you're what I've been waiting for."

Before she can respond, I take her ass cheeks into my grasp and lick her from her pussy to her ass in one long swoop and then go to town. This wasn't my plan, but I couldn't resist either. Roxanne yells out and her arms fall to her sides from the pleasure wracking her body. She rocks her ass into my face and moans.

I'm an ass man, through and through.

Once I have her pussy dripping in my hand is when the fun begins.

"Sit back for me and close your eyes," I tell her, then I take the sash I brought and bring it down over her eyes. I can't wait to have her.

Her hands come up immediately as I tie it behind her head.

"Oh, kinky." She jokes.

"I like a little kink, but this will help you keep your mind off the pain and more on the pleasure. You'll be more focused on the sensations."

"Huh," is all she says.

"If at any time you want me to stop, just tell me and I will." She nods in response. "Ready?" She nods again. "I'm about to ruin any orgasm you have after this. The intensity will make you an addict."

"I'll be the judge of that, playboy."

I scoot behind her, my cock erect and ready. My tip presses against her spine as I slide her hair to her other shoulder and expose her neck. She angles her head, giving me access to kiss along her throat. If Roxanne is willing and able to give this moment to us, to me, then I want to make sure I do everything in my power to give it back to her even better.

My arms come around her curvy waist and I tug her to me, my thighs hugging hers. My lips meet her skin again and I inhale as I drop tongued kisses along the sweet curve of her neck. Her back sandwiches my cock against my stomach in a blanket of warmth. Precum escapes again, this time rubbing against her flesh. Knowing she's wearing my seed makes my cock want to explode. And even though I'm dying to be deep inside of her, I know the wait will be worth it.

"You're going to be filthy by the time we're done. You

fucked me raw without a condom and now I'm going to bareback your ass. My cum will have been in every hole of yours by the time this is over."

This elicits a groan so deep in her chest that it can't be mistaken for anything other than utter bliss. Hell yeah.

I reach for her nipple and her clit at the same time to get the stimulation going, fingering her pussy and playing with her body. I wish I could put my mouth on every part of her at once.

"Don't think about anything. Just feel the sensations and pleasure."

It doesn't take long for her to get worked up again. She's riding my hand like she's humping a pillow, and her ass is massaging into my balls and cock to the point of pain, but it feels so good. I glance down and get lost in us. Flesh to flesh, her sugarplum ass is giving me the most erotic lap dance of my life. I almost don't want to stop, but I do.

"Don't think about anything, Rox." I grab the lube. "Focus on the pleasure. Now lift up for me."

I don't just coat my cock in lube, I also drop a dollop on my finger and then press it to her ass. She tenses as I carefully breach the puckered ring.

"Play with your clit," I instruct. Every woman is different. Not all need clitoral stimulation to have an orgasm with anal sex, though it helps. What is needed most is lube.

When I hear the wetness slipping around her pussy, I say, "Bear down slowly." Once she's seated all the way to my knuckles, she turns her face toward mine. I kiss her mouth with control to set the pace while I play with her breasts. She rides my finger to get comfortable with the intrusive object inside of her. The first time is usually awkward, so I make sure to work her up, otherwise I'm going to tear her pretty good. I pull out and lube up again before inserting two fingers. There's no way she's going to be able to take my cock just yet.

Leaning forward, I kiss the base of her spine and insert three fingers now before I get ready to take her. She clenches around me and takes a deep breath. Goose bumps appear under her skin in response as she slides easily over my digits. Most guys have no patience as it is, but if there's one thing I've learned, it's to take your time when you take an ass.

I tap the side of her outer thigh to signal her to lift, and when she does, I remove my fingers and position the tip of my cock at her entrance.

"If you want it, now's your chance."

Guiding Roxanne's hips, I help her slowly take my tip inside of her. My hands roam her waist, up her spine, and down in circles while I breach past her tender ring. Circulation slows in my dick and it only builds the pleasure. It's taking all my control to not bring her all the way down.

"Rox, I wish you could see how you look right now. Never seen anything more beautiful." I pause, feeling overwhelmed by her presence. I want to paint her in this position, the swoop of her hips and deep arch of her back, all mine for the taking.

She hisses. "I have a good idea what it looks like."

The sound of her voice tells me she's in a bit of distress. I reach for her clit and feel the engorged nub. She cries out, causing her ass to take a little more of my cock.

"Babe. Your pussy lips are huge right now," I tell her, surprised.

"I'd crack a joke, but I can't tell if I'm in pain or if I like this. I feel like I'm stuck in a vortex. I need more of something but don't know what."

I skim my hand to her pussy and find her dripping with desire. It pleases me immensely to know that despite the pain she's in, Roxanne is still allowing the pleasure to override it. I insert two fingers inside her, and she takes another inch or so of my cock in her ass. I'm more than halfway in and it's taking everything in me not to slam her down all the way to the hilt.

She lets out a mewling sound, and my breathing deepens. My fingers pump into her cunt as she rubs her clit over the heel of my hand, unknowingly taking my cock all the way.

"If that feels good, do it," I encourage her. Her juices saturate my hand. A sigh of relief escapes her throat and I know she feels it too.

"You got my cock all the way in your ass, Rox," I whisper against the curve of her neck. She doesn't speak, just nods her head. "You feel incredible. I'm already hungry for you tomorrow. Do you have any idea how much I'm struggling here to not throw you down and fuck you relentlessly?"

"Any other time I would say do it, but not right now."

I stroke her clit with my thumb in a hard and slow fashion while moving my hips back and forth. She grinds into my hand, seeking pleasure she doesn't know how to find through sensations that put her on overload. She doesn't realize that I'm loosening her up, and thanks to the lube, it helps tremendously. I glide in and out of her ass, still somewhat painfully snug, and relish in her tightness.

She tries to lean over and spread her knees on the table, but my strong arms hold her in place. I'm not letting her go anywhere. She moans in pure bliss. She's feeling the intensity climb and she needs more. Her hips are beginning to pump back into mine, her breathing is short and quick.

"Relax on my thighs," I say, and I remove my fingers from her sweet pussy to help guide her back. "Sit back and lean on me." Roxanne cries out at this angle and shudders. Her fingers find her clit and she rubs furiously, falling into the pleasure of her own touch. She pumps back and meets me halfway. She squeaks and cries, eating my cock up on her own now.

I surge slowly into her. Her head rolls back and her mouth falls open. The blindfold allows her to not think and just feel. Taking her hand from her clit, I use two of her fingers with two of mine and insert them into her pussy.

"Feel my cock take you. Feel it, Roxanne."

"Oh my God," she says when I plunge into her ass. "I think I'm close. Oh God. It's so much . . ."

I pause, trying to get myself under control now and

nestle my thighs closer to her. She's a potent blend of sex and passion, and I want a bite of her.

"I want you, Rox. I want you so fucking bad." I kiss her shoulder. My own orgasm is getting closer, and I don't know how much longer I can hold on for. "I'm as deep as I can get inside you and yet I want to be in you deeper. I don't get it."

Her heavy breathing matches mine. "I told you, Brody, I'm yours." Her voice is quiet and low. "Take me how you want." She reaches behind her and places her hands on my thighs for leverage. "Feed it to me."

Chills run down my spine. Being inside Roxanne and hearing her say those words sends me off the edge. I've had anal more times than I can count, but none have felt as sensual as this. Or as intimate.

Without wasting another second, I bring us to heights she's never soared, playing with her pussy like my hand is her personal vibrator. I take her hard and find my release. She's got a good rhythm now and isn't afraid to take more of me when she wants to.

I love it.

"When it's time for you to come, I don't want you to hold back."

"I never do."

"This is different, Rox. It's going to hit you harder. Just let go and take my cock. Make all the noise you want, baby."

With one arm folded across her hips, I give her pussy attention while I surge into her ass with a craving I need to get me off. Keeping her body against mine, I wrap my fingers around her throat and squeeze. I apply pressure and choke her just enough for her orgasm to surge up her spine.

She's about to blow up from pleasure and never want to come down.

"Brody, oh my God, Brody." She bucks harder, riding the high.

"I told you, babe, just let go."

She gasps, her ass clenching around my cock. Her strangled cries echo throughout the house.

"It feels too good. I'm almost scared." She whimpers.

"Be free with me." A few more thrusts and we're sailing into the abyss. "Be with me and just let go."

Roxanne sings soprano, shaking as she comes. She's squirting again and she doesn't even know it. I glance down and watch as her wetness soaks the fabric of the pool table, causing it to shift into different shades of green. I bite into her back, hungry to make her keep spilling like that.

"That's right, give it to me. Come for me." Watching her shoot her pleasure on to the table sets me off like a rocket. I air guitar the fuck out of her clit and watch the liquid splash all over.

"Oh fuck, Rox. Oh fuck. Rox, I'm coming."

My balls tighten up and blood rises before I can stop it. I shoot into her without reserve and exhale in gratification. My semen explodes against the walls of her ass and pushes her orgasm to make her breathless. She contracts and flexes, her body convulsing from the superior sex between us.

"More, give me more. Brody. Oh God, keep playing with my pussy, I'm coming so hard."

Roxanne throws out a string of curse words, her pleasure bleeding into me. Her nails score my thighs and I'm pretty sure she broke the skin. I release my load entirely inside of her, orgasming so hard I hold my breath. She's leaking all over the table and down her thighs. My balls are soaked with her release, and now she's leaking from her ass. I have no idea what I'm gonna tell the guys when they see it, but I don't really care.

"Is this what it feels like to kiss the stars?"

"Yes," I say without hesitation.

"Then I never want to come down."

Leaning forward, I carefully take her down to the table as I mount her from behind. There's a caveman part of me that wants me to make her completely mine. I release everything I have, straining against her ass, giving her my seed until I'm empty. Roxanne's knee slides up the table, willingly giving me her body.

I'm completely spent.

I pull out gently so it doesn't hurt, then turn her over. We're a mess of sex and my cum is everywhere. I've never been this filthy from sex before, and that's because not many women seem to care for it. But not Roxy. Her orgasm is soaking the table, and whatever body parts touch it blends with my pleasure. Now that I really think about it, I might have to buy a whole new pool table for the guys.

I remove the blindfold. Roxanne searches for me immediately.

Her hazel eyes make me a goner. Clarity glistens with unspoken acknowledgment. She exhales a breath of relief, her fingers tremble in my view. There's an intimacy one can't explain in the aftershock.

Roxanne spreads her legs for me and reaches her arms out. I collapse on top of her in a heap and slowly kiss her lips with gratitude. She doesn't move or pull away. She returns the kiss with the same tenderness. Her legs tangle with mine as she exhales through her nose, her lips not giving up.

Some of the greatest artists in history were inspired by a muse, an enigma for the creative minds. Roxanne is a burst of energy that sparks my mind. I want to cover us in what we made together so it's painted on her. My body hums to the vibrations of euphoria, but desperate for the warmth of nothing more than her naked body. We ride the wave, rocking together in a state of harmony. I relish in the small twitches of gratification that continue to prickle throughout our bodies. This isn't my first time with anal, but it is for her, so I know how she's feeling.

Roxanne needs me, she just doesn't know it.

The truth is, I need her too.

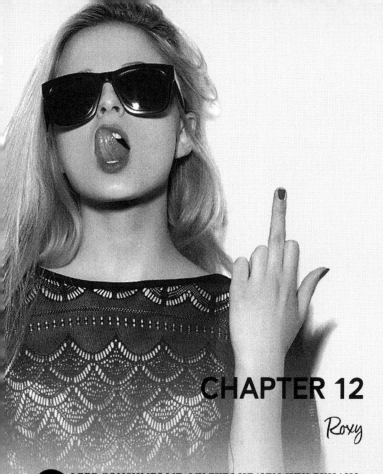

CHAPTER 12

Roxy

SLEEP CONSUMES ME, MY EYES HEAVY WITH EXHAUStion.

I need to yawn, but I'm too tired and burrow close to the source of heat at my back. I bask in a blanket of warmth, nestled partially under a naked body. Strong arms surround me in a cage of protection.

Consciousness fades in and out as I try to remember where I am, whose bed I'm in, whose cock is sandwich between my ass cheeks. There's a cell phone ringing and vibrating at the same time that's distracting me from falling into a deep slumber. I feel like I just fell asleep. My eyes sting. The urge to stretch is strong, like my muscles need it. The ringing ensues and the night flashes before my closed lids. It all comes back to me now.

Brody.

Fucking Brody.

A man. A myth. A legend all rolled into a fine fucking package if I ever saw one. He's gonna be a hard one-night stand to top.

The things he made me experience were on another level. Some of which were a first. Not even I could bring myself to orgasm the way he did, and I'm pretty good at knowing how to sex myself up. Brody made the pleasure feel infinite. I don't know how he did it and I don't care to know. Every part of him was actively involved, and I think that's what upped the ante on my end. He was attentive. Extremely attentive. He brought out that need I hadn't realized I'd been stowing away, and once I latched on, I was hooked. The thought stirs my blood while I lie half asleep. Not even sex on ecstasy compares to Brody. Though, I wonder what he'd feel like under that haze.

Wait until I tell Estelle about the squirting. I was so embarrassed. I thought I was peeing at first. But when I heard Brody's excitement, it made me unstoppable. So, I let go and . . . squirted. If I'd stopped then, I would've lost my orgasm, and I wasn't going to allow that to happen. That was a first for me, and so was the anal sex.

I'd been low key dying to try anal for a little while now.

I love a good dildo, but it wasn't what I wanted for my first time. I wanted the real thing, and I wanted to stimulate both erogenous zones, but I couldn't when I was focusing so much.

In comes Brody and blows me away. It was everything I could've ever wanted and more.

The ringing proceeds and my eyes flutter open. It's my cell phone. Briefly I wonder if it's Estelle calling me. I lick my dry lips and turn over, rolling into Brody's big chest. After the anal sex, I was finished. I could barely hold my eyes open after the orgasm, let alone walk on two legs.

And then all he wanted to do was kiss. But man, his lips were potent, erotic, slow, a lover's speed. Brody scooped me up into his arms and carried me down the hall into a pitch-black room, where he spooned me for the rest of the night naked under a blanket.

The tip of my nose skims his throat. He smells delicious, like he's been working in a field under the sun. Brody rolls on to his back, taking me with him, and wedges a thigh between mine. I like how he moves with my flow and adapts.

A smile spreads across my face he can't see. I giggle quietly. "Sorry, hunk. I need my cell."

I reach for the sound and see the home screen light up on a table by his bed. I push up on my elbows and then stretch across Brody's chest. My breasts drag near his beard, his fine hair tickling my nipple. I squint at the bright light and lower it. Brody appears in the corner of my eye. He's watching me as I swipe open the home screen and read the text messages from my agent, Von, and not Estelle like I assumed.

I frown as I scroll through the repeat text messages to call him. My first thought is that something happened to my family. I try not to overreact, but to me it's the only logical reason for the number of urgent messages he sent.

Or the paparazzi are about to ruin my life and Von wanted to warn me first.

"Rox, put the phone away and come back to bed. Whomever it is can wait. I'm not ready to wake up with you yet."

I pause to meet his gaze, liking the sound of his words. Brody's hands roam my naked body, encouraging me to listen. Except my phone goes off again, ringing this time, and I swipe to answer. I can't not respond to him now.

"It's my agent," I whisper to Brody before I bring the phone to my ear. "What do you want, Von? I'm trying to get my beauty rest so I can look forever young."

"That's what Botox is for. Where the hell have you been? Never mind, it doesn't matter."

Von sounds like he's been up for two days straight running on cocaine and caffeine. I pull my phone away to check the time. I groan inwardly. I'm not a morning person.

"It's five-thirty in the morning. You couldn't wait until at least the sun has risen to call me?"

"There's no rest for the wicked. Where are you?"

"I'm not sure, I think Santa Monica." Brody leans

forward and tugs my nipple into his mouth. I gasp. "What's with the urgency?"

"The urgency is that I got you an audition."

I perk up and Brody pulls more into his mouth. He flattens his tongue and sucks my nipple enough to leave a hickey.

"An audition? I got an audition? Where? For what?"

Hope filters through my hazy thoughts. It's been a few years since the reality show, and I haven't had much work, not for lack of trying either.

I want more, but no one will take me seriously. Not after the show. Estelle and I had made a pact during the last season to let loose and not tell the crew. We wanted to make it memorable. They gave us an inch, and we took a mile. We got away with murder that summer.

While those years brought Estelle into my life and the opportunity to live abroad, occasionally I find myself regretting ever considering it in the first place. It's left me with a title of shame perched above my head and the ability to feel like I'm overlooked and viewed as talentless.

Being a Bardot comes with its own set of disadvantages, and of them is being born into Hollywood. I'm more than a pretty face who can pose for a picture. I take pride in my body and love who I am. But I want to be known for more than headlining the first Victoria's Secret Plus Size Holiday Fashion Show. I don't want people to only see Bardot Studios when they look at me. I want to act. And one day I want to own a business.

"Ah, sleeping beauty is awake now."

My eyes shoot to Brody. I want to say something sarcastic about him being my knight and shining armor, but I don't. I've waited for this call from Von and now that I got it, I don't want to let it go.

"If you kiss me in the right place, I wake up." I can't help myself. Von laughs. "What's the audition for? And if you tell me it's for another ad campaign, I might fire you."

Von goes silent. "You're not home, are you?"

"Of course not."

"It's a Tuesday, Roxy."

"And? I can't have one-night stands on certain days of the week? Where's that mail order bride of yours?"

He rightfully ignores me. "What's his name? Do anything I should be concerned about that could end up in the news?"

"I can't remember his name." Brody smacks my ass cheek and I giggle. I'm pretty sure I'll never forget him. "But he violated me in all the right places," I tell my agent. "So, I might place a gold star right next to his name in my book."

"Listen, Roxy. Don't fuck this up. It's what you've been waiting for."

My chest tightens at his words. "How so?"

Von isn't one for small talk and gets right to business. He knows I'm desperate to do something with my life other than fall back on my name. I just don't know what I want because I'm eager to try new things. I want to experience as much as I can in this lifetime.

I want a lot of things. I just don't know how to incorporate something I love when what I'm supposed to love has been chosen for me since the day I was born.

I once broached the idea of having my own cooking show after a season of filming in Italy. Von had said unless I planned to cook naked no one was going to watch. I guess for now film is where it is and the secrets I took home from top chefs will only be sampled in my kitchen.

"I'm sending you an email now with the details. The studio is already way behind in production and it's making everyone act like assholes because their money is burning by the second. Casting is having trouble finding a female lead to work with the actor. They set up another round of auditions in an attempt to find her quickly. Filming is set to begin . . ." I hear Von shuffling papers in the background. I swear this guy doesn't sleep. "In less than two weeks."

My brows rise. That's not good. That means everyone is going to be high-strung and overstressed.

"Maybe the male lead is the problem."

Brody tugs my nipple with his teeth. "Ow," I mouth, and a smirk appears in his eyes. He releases me. I playfully slap him and then roll over on to my back. He follows me and climbs between my legs. He drops his whole body right over mine. His head rests on my belly, and for the first time that I can remember, I'm completely at ease with someone using my pooch as a pillow. Strong arms wrap around my sides. My fingers thread his hair softly.

"He probably is," Von says.

"Who is it? What's the actor's name?"

"No idea, and I don't care. You're testing with other actresses, or wannabes, anyway. You won't be the only one there."

"Be nice, Von. You were a wannabe once."

Naturally, he ignores me if it doesn't benefit him. "Okay, sent. Check your email ASAP and start reading. You'll find the script and the Cliffs Notes. You'll need to be there in an hour."

My eyes widen. "An hour? Um . . .There's one little problem."

"I expected that with you. What is it?"

"I don't have my car and I went to the Sunset Den last night."

Von's quiet. "You're supposed to stay away from that place, Roxy."

He's not pleased, but with good reason. The Sunset Den has been around since the seventies. It has an infamous history of wild parties and overdoses.

It's my favorite place to hang.

"I'm supposed to do a lot of things, none of which sound fun when someone's telling me to do them."

"Going to a place where you were arrested is asking for trouble."

"I like trouble. Keeps me feeling alive."

"Want to feel alive? Go take some MDMA on one of the private islands your parents own and don't tell anyone. I don't know why I keep you as a client."

"You're still making money off me or else you would've let me go by now."

A smile he can't see spreads across my face. He's not serious, but that's only because I've known him since I was a teenager. My jobs have been few and far between, but when they are, I bank off them . . . And so does my agent. He knows I'm right.

A car door slams in the background. "Need me to send a car?" he asks.

I clench my eyes shut, trying to process everything. Most of my jobs have been for catalog modeling and not something I had to audition in person for. The others required a headshot or a strut down a makeshift catwalk. None of which I had to perform as another person, or with another person.

Anxiety fills me and I try to push it down. I tell myself this is what I've been waiting for, a moment like this to prove myself. But now that I have it, I'm suddenly giving it a second thought and wondering if I really do want this. If I have what it takes.

"No, I'll get there. I'll call Estelle and she can bring me clothes. What's your take on the script? What genre are we talking about, and is there nudity? I know you have an opinion or else you wouldn't suggest I audition."

"You know that guy who wrote *The Notebook*? It's one of his books that was optioned for film."

"You're kidding me." I'm no longer filled with anxiety. "I know him. Well, of him."

I've read many of his novels and sincerely love them. I just have an aversion to the way he makes me feel when the book is over. I'm left reeling with too many feelings from the pile of sorrow he manifested from his mind, and I don't know how to function after that.

I can't wait to see which book it is now and if I've read it or not.

"Even better. Just get there as quick as you can. Being fashionably late doesn't always work in your favor, and after speaking with the studio, I can tell you they feel the same."

"Aye, aye, captain."

"This last-minute audition wasn't my idea. I'm not sure you're even fit for the job."

I frown, trying not to be offended by his words. It sobers up my playful mood. "It wasn't?"

"You were requested."

I stare into the dark, my mind running a mile a minute. Someone specifically asked for me?

This audition just got a lot more interesting.

"Who asked for me?"

"Don't know, don't care. Consider this a step ahead of the competition."

"Shit. I don't even have underwear on."

"You're testing with other actors, not fucking them, Roxy. Go commando if you need to, just don't screw this opportunity up. Every other gig you've wanted has rejected you before you were permitted to even audition.

Now someone wants you. They're going to specifically be watching you. Call me when it's over."

I swallow thickly and my phone pings. "Your email just came through." I pause, grateful for this chance despite the banter between us. "Thanks, Von."

"Thank me when you get the job."

The line goes dead and my screen turns dark. I let my phone go and it slides off the pillow on to the bed.

"Let me guess." Brody nuzzles my pelvis. His voice is groggy but it's kind of cozy. "Duty calls."

"I thought you fell back asleep."

Brody doesn't play fair and dips his head between my spread thighs, trying to nudge my pussy lips open with his nose. He presses a kiss to my pussy and it wakes me up. As much as I want him to keep going, Von's right. And deep down I know he is. I won't get a first opportunity twice, so I need to make the best of this.

"I have an audition I can't really afford to skip." I realize I probably sound like most young adults desperate for fame living in Hollywood. It kind of bothers me a little, but I let it go. There's no time for emotions when it's time to work. "Unfortunately, I have to leave."

"Why unfortunate?"

"Because I actually wanted you, but I need to call my friend and get a move on. I don't think I have time for your sex."

"You're a hit it and run type, aren't you?"

"Sometimes."

"Mostly." He corrects me.

My cheeks burn. I totally wanted Brody for leftovers. But I'm wearing our bodily fluids and I haven't looked in a mirror since I left my house last night. I need to wash up the best I can and make sure there's no evidence left on me for someone to point out.

"Your sex tells a story."

"And?"

"I only have time for a song."

"Rox?"

I'm quiet. I don't say anything for a beat because I'm too lost in my thoughts. "Yeah?"

"That might be one of the best compliments I've ever gotten." Brody rests his head on my inner thigh, his fingers drawing crazy eights on my stomach. "Call your friend and get your shit situated. Wherever she's at is going to take her at least twenty minutes to get to us, and what are you going to do in the meantime? Pace my floor? I could give you at least three orgasms in that time." Brody leans up and pushes my knees back to sit between my legs. My gaze falls to his erection.

I chuckle. "Already hard, I see."

"Babe, I've been hard all night lying next to you. And I'm probably going to be hard when you leave too."

I reach for my phone and text Estelle. We're each other's go-to when the moment strikes. Codependency at its finest.

I watch and wait, eager for the orgasm I know Brody

will make sure I have, and for the audition I'm about to go on. He spits in his hand and then strokes himself, rolling his hips against mine so the tip touches my clit.

Thankfully, Estelle responds quickly and I don't have to call her. I give her a brief rundown and her excitement is clear in her response. She tells me to drop a pin for my location since technically I don't know where I'm at and she'll get me in twenty-five minutes.

I tell Brody.

He grins.

CHAPTER 13

Roxy

WITH LITTLE TIME TO SPARE, I LOOKED UP REviews on the book—both good and bad—and read them to Estelle while she drove us like a bat out of hell back to the city.

It was still early, so the traffic hadn't been too bad yet. I read lines to her from the manuscript to get an idea for the role, and we broke down the Cliffs Notes Von had sent me. Her excitement was contagious, and it gave me the confidence to think I have what it takes. She's happy for me and can't wait to see how it goes.

Estelle hasn't worked much since the show, and while I have, it hasn't been anything this grand. She's also cool with living off her trust, so she's not too eager to grow up yet. Her words. I don't blame her. I still don't know what I want to do either other than make a living for myself without the help of the Bardot name.

We didn't have time to discuss where the truck came from she picked me up in. I'm fairly certain it's the same truck of the guy she went home with, which surprises me. Men are stupid about who drives their truck, and they just met. But we already have plans to talk about our adventurous night this afternoon. Apparently, hers was just as wild and we need to spill to each other. I didn't have the guts to tell her about the squirting yet, but I'm going to over brunch in Melrose Square. I want to see her initial reaction.

Life is so much more entertaining when you have a bestie by your side.

Taking a deep breath, I exit the elevator on the fifth level and glance around. Floor-to-ceiling windows line the vast office space with a remarkable view of the rising sun. It's better than the view from my house. There are three doors, and behind one of them is where I assume the audition is being held. If this goes well, it will be due to a miracle.

I try to push down the nerves that just barreled into me from the realization of where I am and what I'm doing. This is the real deal. I have one shot to make an impression.

There's rows of chairs lined up against the wall, a few of them filled with familiar faces, none of which I actually know personally. I offer a smile in way of greeting, then take one of the empty seats and pull up the manuscript on my cell phone. I spend my time trying to emulate the director's vision. I feel like I have a good grasp on the tone, and I practice the lines in my head like how I imagine they'd go. Aspiring candidates are called one by one, some testing longer than others. Only two so far are asked to remain and take a seat after, while the majority walk to the elevator I came up on.

I wait with my heart pounding in my throat for my name to be called. Despite being raised in front of a camera, I still get nervous. The adrenaline hits me from both sides, and I low key crave it. I want to run away, but I want to run headfirst more.

With the first audition, it's crucial to have at least one prepared monologue. Emotive and gripping. I need to be able to show an array of emotions in a very short amount of time. We're talking about seconds to make a lasting impact. Everything down to my hair, how I walk into the room, and the clothes I wear are considered in those moments. I'm not dressed to impress, which already puts me at a disadvantage. I probably look like I just rolled in off the streets.

Which I did.

Estelle had called when she was on her way and said she didn't have a change of clothes for me. I took one of Brody's flannel shirts and wore it like a dress. I'm a tall woman, but he's taller and bigger. His shirt hits me at mid-thigh and I had to roll up the sleeves. My breasts are too large though, so I left the first couple of buttons open. I'm wearing my stilettos from the night before.

"My shirt looks better on you," he'd said before he tried removing it. *"I can't keep my hands off you."*

Brody.

I shiver thinking about how he must be a figment of my imagination because there's no way he's real.

Knowing Von, he probably put in a call to fabricate a lie about me just flying back into town and to disregard my appearance because I wasn't prepared. He likes to cover his hairy ass any which way he can.

Still, I can't give less than my best if I want to get a callback.

And I really want it.

I read over the scenes until my name is called. I stand with butterflies in my stomach and walk toward the woman holding the door open for me. She has a clipboard held close to her chest and speaks into the microphone of her black headset as she eyes me. I swallow thickly and put on my show business face the Bardot name seems to come equipped with since birth.

Here we go, I think to myself as I step into the room. I push my shoulders back and lift my chin, then turn my attention immediately toward the room of people. My eyes light up and I can't stop the huge smile from spreading across my face. The genuine happiness I feel is exhilarating, and I decide not to push it down to be professional but to instead let it exude from me to show how appreciative I am to be here.

I'm not naïve. Luck has been on my side my entire life. But it wasn't luck that got me here this morning. I blush from the onset of opportunity that rushes through me as realization hits of how much I want this. To be given this chance is not something I want to take for granted.

Someone saw something in me . . . And now I want them to remember me.

There are two six-foot tables with three people at each and a camera stationed right in the middle. I know from experience that the people standing near the wall are studio executives and maybe even the financiers of the film. I make eye contact with each of them before I come to a stop in front of a background screen and over the red X tapped to the floor. Two of them are familiar faces, and we silently acknowledge the other. My knees are anxious to bounce from nerves. Taking a deep breath, I separate the emotional aspect from the professional, knowing that alone will carry me further, and then exhale my last fear.

The men at the table are attractive. Von didn't know who the lead actor was, and as I look at the males before me, I'm not sure myself. There are three potentials who I feel would fit the role. I try to figure out which of them it could be, but it's not easy when all eyes are on me. The back of my neck prickles with awareness and I reach up to rub it away. There's a pair of eyes burning a hole into the side of my head, I just don't know who they belong to and I don't want to look away like I'm distracted.

"Look right at the camera. State your name and where you're from."

I drop my arm and get to business. "My name is Roxanne Bardot. I live in Los Angeles."

The guy in a plain white crew neck shirt behind the camera speaks again. I think he might be the casting director. "And what is the name of the film you're auditioning for?"

"*Under the Lemon Tree.*"

I'm acutely aware the movie director and producer are here watching too, but I try to not let it get to me.

"How old are you?"

"I'm twenty-one."

"And why are you here?"

"I'm auditioning for the lead role of Gwen."

I'm handed a few pieces of loose paper containing the scene they want me to test. I quickly scan over it, trying to focus on the words and not on the pounding in my chest. Under normal circumstances I would have my own script, but since they're aware I'm a last-minute casting call, they offer me theirs. My hands tremble and the papers shake, so I take a deep breath and steady myself.

I glance up and look at the camera, then at the bigwigs standing in the room.

"I'm not sure what you were made aware of, Ms. Bardot, but the lead actor is here today. Once we run lines with you, we'll have River test with you next. If we like what we see, you'll wait outside with the other callbacks until we're ready for you again."

My gaze immediately finds River Bolton sitting at the end of one of the tables. His eyes bore into mine flagrantly in a room full of people. He's the one who's been watching me.

My stomach tightens and my heart climbs to my throat. The first thought that crosses my mind is that he looks like a jerk with a bad attitude. His shoulders are stiff and his hands are folded on the table next to the stacked papers. His knee bounces relentlessly. I don't blink as I watch him with the same intensity he puts out. I feel like he's trying to throw me off kilter, but the impulse to run toward him is stronger.

If this is his attempt to intimidate me, then he's going to have to try harder. I've had lots of practice with my younger brother, Brooklyn, and his hormonal rages when we were teens.

"Sounds good," is all I say with a beaming smile. "Ready when you are," I lie.

I hear the casting director talking, but I can't tear my gaze away from River. He's undeniably the second most handsome man I've seen in the past twenty-four hours. He's got hair like a young Brad Pitt and an angular face with prominent brows. With his striking jewel-like eyes, he's one of those discreet Hollywood heartthrobs who has been linked to gorgeous women but rarely seen with them in public.

Heat spans through my chest. A bite of exhilaration tingles my skin. He's definitely not someone I'd imagine as the lead for this movie. He typically plays the vigilante in action and suspense films, wielding guns and getting caught in the crossfire, saving innocents from death.

The kind of stuff that doesn't appeal to me.

A woman comes forward with a black clapperboard in her hand. She opens it in front of my face and then turns to the camera for the next order. My heart is pounding in my chest knowing any second—

She snaps it shut and says, "Take one."

The casting director looks at the crinkled papers in his grasp and starts to read lines. I blink rapidly and free my mind of everything else but this moment.

I lift my script and recite my lines, pulling on the emotion I personally feel is needed for the tone of the role. All I want is to impress them with every fiber in my body and give them what they're looking for.

"Cut."

CHAPTER 14

Roxy

I GLANCE UP WITH WIDE EYES. I HADN'T EXPECTED TO stop just yet. A man in a three-piece suit stands behind the camera mumbling under his breath to the casting director.

"Do it again." The casting director looks at me. "But turn to the side this time so I can see you in a different profile. When you're done reading, do it again from the other side."

I nod, and the woman snaps the clapperboard for the second take. This direction tells me I need to move more and not stand in one place. My damn nerves are getting to me.

Knowing this is my second chance at the same scene, I pull on more feelings I didn't know I was capable of and perform my heart out to a room full of strangers and a video camera. I run my fingers through my knotted hair and tug on the ends, using it as a prop. Angrily pleading my lines, I step forward and my jaw trembles from unshed tears. By the time I turn to the opposite side and repeat my lines, tears are falling down my cheeks as I evoke real emotion developed for the character I'm playing.

"Okay, cut."

The director turns to me again. "Read over the last scene while I watch this over."

My heart thumps wildly in my chest. Being asked to read another scene is a very good sign.

They don't wait for a response and get to work, rewinding my performance and viewing it with creased brows and narrowed eyes. I flip the pages over and lick my dry lips. I can feel River watching me intently, but I don't give him the attention even though I want to. Failure is not an option, and I need to succeed with this next test if I want to run lines with him. Which I really do.

"Change of plans. River, I need you up there now," the director says. My eyes widen and roam over the room of people. This means he likes what he saw, and now he wants to see more. I'm beaming like a fool inside even though I'm about to have a heart attack. "Read the last page together," he adds.

River stands and smooths his hands down the front of his jeans. He runs his fingers through his dirty blond hair and it falls perfectly over his cheekbones in a nice arc.

My body awakens as he walks toward me. River must have been squished sitting in that chair, because the man is large. I'm momentarily stunned and hold my breath. He swaggers closer in casual clothes, his long legs eating up the space between us. Our eyes lock and my lips part as he nears. I take a small step back, holding the script close to my chest. His presence doesn't go unnoticed. The whole room is watching him.

I'm acutely aware every second of my time here is being watched and recorded. River is my on-screen love interest, which means we need to have the harmony and pull between us before he even walks up to me. It's common sense the chemistry between two actors is what sells a film. Without the right cast, a film or any television show will flop. There have been times when a movie didn't make it past the casting phase and the whole production was shut down because the right people weren't found.

I need to sell us.

It also means I don't need to hold back how striking I really find him in person. I rake a gaze down his husky body and like what I see. My eyes lower. River is just as good-looking as the man I had last night . . . and this morning. I'm still coming down from the high of Brody. My cheeks flush thinking about how he had made me his one last time. I never got a fresh pair of panties, and now I'm wearing his clothes. Brody wanted to text me his cell before I left, but I shook my head and smiled. I don't exchange numbers on a first fuck.

River stops in front of me. He's a big-boned guy and towers in muscle from head to toe. There's a slight level of intimidation from his size. I feel small next to him, which isn't an easy feat.

He doesn't say anything as we swap glances. His gaze roams my face as he takes me in. I do the same, trying to get acquainted with him without talking. One side of his mouth lifts in a half smile, and I relax my shoulders.

"You good?" he says.

I smile and hold his stare. "I'm good."

River and I turn to the camera for the next take. The director uses his hands to speak. "Read the script over before we start, Roxanne. If we need another take, it's simply because we're behind schedule and need to make sure we make the right choice. We'll probably want to see it from a few angles."

I nod. No pressure or anything.

Glancing down, I wash away any thought crossing my mind and only focus on the typewriter font in the center of the page. We're given no more than sixty seconds to get in tune with the scene and comprehend the dialogue being conveyed. Taking a deep breath, I attempt to steady my nerves and the fluttering in my stomach. The woman with the clapperboard waits for her cue as she stands off to the side.

River and I exchange a quick glance. He looks away and I pick up the script. He probably has it memorized as I just now notice he doesn't have it with him.

"Take three. River Bolton and Roxanne Bardot. *Under The Lemon Tree*. Action."

The word "action" snaps us both into place. We're mentally transported to the backyard of a Victorian home overlooking a lake. We're two ex-lovers in a passionate disagreement over how their daughter should be raised. My character is the one who walked away, and now she's back asking for a place in their child's life. River's character is reluctant to give it to her because of her past addictions, which caused her to walk out in the first place.

River begins his dialogue, and I hold the paper prepared to recite my lines. I know if I deliver the emotion properly, then it won't matter that I'm reading off a script so closely, or that I'm completely unprepared.

My hands tremble as I imagine myself in the character's position. It's a heartbreaking tale that I resonate with. I'm not naïve enough to deny my addictions, but now I'm playing a character with the same problems and it's disturbing my reality. There's a part of me that wants to hold back, to hide the truth of how far one's addictions can truly take them.

River's voice rises and I step back only to rebut the character's argument. A surge of adrenaline flashes through me. It gives me a newfound confidence, and I decide to bite back. If he's brash, then I'm hasty. As I match him, I find myself moving closer to River. He glares down at me with fire in his eyes. It only spurs me more to dig deep and mimic the feelings he gives. If we're two parents, then he must understand my plea, right? I raise the paper with shaky hands, reading the lines while feeling the pent-up tension from River as he paces the floor in front of me. He's quick with his dialogue, and it makes me work harder in return to keep the scene moving and remain intense like him. The emotion he evokes from his words to protect their child makes my heart race with excitement. I like this push and pull. River performs the lines like he's rehearsed them a million times with ease. It makes me want to be as good as him.

My voice starts to shake. I stay focused as best I can, but my thoughts start to slip when I hear a sneeze and then a cell phone ring. Mid-sentence River notices the papers flittering in my hand. My nerves are getting to me and I'm sure he senses it.

His expression transforms into what I can only describe as an angry, protective father. Subconsciously I think how extraordinary it is for one to be able to shift their entire being into a character's personality in the blink of an eye. It inspires me to see if I can expand my capabilities.

But then River pulls out a pair of sunglasses. He takes a few steps away from me and props his hands on his hips, giving me his back. I study him, trying to gage his next move. He's equal parts antagonistic and appealing. His shoulders are stiff as he huffs under his breath loud enough for me to hear. Confusion mares my face. I quickly glance down and skim the dialogue in search of an answer.

I come up with nothing.

My mind races back to the words I just ran with him when it suddenly hits me. Dread forms in my stomach.

Shit.

River is doing the one thing I struggle with.

He's improvising.

CHAPTER 15

River

I DON'T KNOW WHAT'S COME OVER ME.

One minute I'm running lines with Roxanne, and the next I'm veering off course to create our own path of dialogue.

Her hands were shaking. She looked like a disaster. And I was sick of revisiting the same dialogue and getting nowhere. She didn't seem like she'd crumble, so I threw a wrench to see if she would dodge it or catch it.

Improvising has always made my balls shrivel up. I don't particularly care for it, but I know it's also a way of showing what you're capable of under pressure. Most often it pays off, a few times it hasn't. I'm no comedian, and I had no idea if she could ad-lib or not, but I took the chance anyway. She seems like she could handle it.

Running my fingers through my hair, I spin on my heels. The lines are boring me and I'm getting frustrated. I crowd Roxanne's space to see if she's intimidated. Fear is the last thing I'd want for a female to feel around me, particularly my co-star, but she needs to be able to handle me and not be scared. The roles I've played in the past have required me to bulk up on equal parts muscle and fat. One of my exes once told me I appear more menacing than I really am. She basically had said I'm a giant stuffed lemur.

I'm going to choke slam my agent for insisting I take this role.

I release a sigh that seems to fit well for the scene we're doing and meet Roxanne's scathing glare. Her eyes are glossy, and she reeks of alcohol and overly expensive perfume. There's not enough intensity from the manuscript like I get from a thriller and I'm starting to lose my edge. I guess hindsight is twenty-twenty and this is what I get for attempting to play a role in a romantic drama. I don't have the patience for it. I need to feel her rage, her passion, the power fueling her words in order to continue, otherwise I feel too much like a sitting duck. We've been sitting on this production for too long now. None of the actresses who've auditioned did anything out of the ordinary other than read the script flawlessly. They we're perfect, just not for me.

The room is completely silent while the crew watches. No one makes a sound. Roxanne's hand trembles as she yells her dialogue. She hasn't moved from her initial stance, despite her admirable performance. But I need her to engage with me more to see if this could really work out. The casting director already has someone else in mind from today's audition. She's waiting in the lobby with the other callbacks. But I like the fire in Roxanne's eyes and the energy she gives off. It makes me want to go further with her to see what she's got. She's not your typical actress and hasn't stared in any real roles. She was on some show with her friend and walked in fashion shows or some shit.

Gripping her wrist, I pull her close and a jolt of life flows from her to me. Roxanne stalls for a split second, then lifts the script to read it with her free hand. She won't find what she's looking for.

Her body is soft against mine that I almost stumble myself. She's got a matter of seconds to counter me before she blows her chance, and she knows it. I already have the part, she doesn't.

Panic fills her eyes, and her large breasts heave against the raggedy, ugly flannel shirt she's wearing when an idea strikes me.

My gaze lowers and I step closer, invading her space. I put an arm around the small of her back. She releases a little gasp but comes to me naturally. Roxanne stands on the tips of her toes and leans against me. I find it incredibly tempting and hold her close because I can get away with it.

She's a knockout. I'm not blind. Roxanne warms the blood in my cock. Seeing the oversized shirt on her, she looks like she just rolled out of bed and threw it on last minute to race over here. Her milky cleavage peeks out from under her long, messy hair laying over her chest. I briefly wonder if she's wearing a bra. My gaze drops to her hardened nipples and my thoughts drift further.

My next move isn't part of the script, but it looks like Roxanne wore her boyfriend's shirt to the audition. I don't allow myself to think much but instead act on impulse. I pretend as if she were my real ex and I'm seeing her look like she just had sex and is glowing from it. We're each other's past love, so I assume there must be some old feelings left unresolved. Jealousy is concealed and a child is used as a scapegoat. I'm not entirely sure this aspect is in the original manuscript, and I don't care. The story is missing lust.

"You're not seeing our child while wearing another man's shirt," I say, devising a hidden agenda for my character. "She's already confused enough wondering where her mother is." I keep her close and let her feel my anger. "We don't need her thinking she's got two fathers now."

Lifting my chin, I wait for Roxanne to counter me. A jealous ex with baby mama drama always adds to the tension.

A moment of clarity forms in her pretty eyes. My chest tightens as I hold my breath hoping she defies me. Seconds are left before we hear the director yell cut if she doesn't make a move.

Roxanne blinks and someone else emerges.

"Confused because you wouldn't let me see her," Roxanne rebuts through her teeth. "You give me excuse after excuse. I can't even Facetime her!"

She yanks away from me and narrows her eyes. Roxanne is instantly fuming and a part of me is thrilled. She makes it interesting to play with.

"The truth has a funny way of coming out of the closet," she adds. Her words are sour. "You still want me," she says proudly. "That's your problem." There's a sad longing in her eyes that calls out to me. The crossfire between two lovers who can't have each other so they fight instead just to keep the other around.

"You have a drug problem," I state, trying to use the envy I showed as protectiveness for a child. She rears back.

"Used to. I *used* to have a drug problem. As if you're some saint and completely sober. You don't drink? At all?"

I stand taller, insulted. "I'm sober enough to raise our child. You can't be trusted to do the right thing for yourself, let alone a kid. Do you even know who her favorite singer is right now?"

She pauses, her eyes looking back and forth at mine. Her brows furrow.

"Harry Styles?"

It takes everything in me to not laugh. I roll my lips between my teeth and press down to keep the laughter in. I was waiting for her to curse me out, but she threw me a curve ball instead. The way she said his name tells me she was trying to figure out who a young child could be interested in now.

"Eddie Vedder," I answer.

She throws her arms in the air and drops them to her thighs. She almost laughs but hides it well. "That was a trick question. You knew I'd get it wrong, you selfish son of a bitch."

"Not my problem she takes after you and changes her mind every time she blinks."

She shakes her head as she gathers her thoughts. "You used our daughter as a weapon for the way I make your dick feel." She marches up to me unabashed. Her hair is wild, like she didn't brush it before she left the house. "You have no right. None. If you want to stick your pecker in me so I can see her, then I'm yours, baby."

I angle my head to the side. My eyes roam her face and land on her mouth. She snorts in disgust noticing my gaze, and it makes me weirdly satisfied. I didn't see her taking that route, and it impresses me.

Roxanne grabs my shirt, and much to my surprise, tears fill her eyes. "Please, I miss her. I haven't seen her in weeks. Let me see her at least sleeping."

Beauty like Roxanne's is dangerous. The woman is gorgeous. It comes naturally, even in the state of distress she's in. The way she walked through the doors, her haphazard clothes, sky-high heels that are evidently from the night before, altered the whole audition.

We just hadn't known it.

Tears fall down her cheeks. Streaked mascara gives her raccoon eyes. But I see the longing in her stare. I hear the wanting in her plea, the need in her body. I feel it in my gut and take a deep breath.

This feels right.

Roxanne drops her head to my chest, whimpering, clutching my shirt in her fist. I lean in and kiss the top of her head. My fingers get lost in her ratty hair. Of all things that get to me, I can't stand to see a woman cry.

"Please," she says, bringing me back to the moment. "You can even stand next to me while I look at her. I don't even have to touch her."

In all the years I've been acting and had to improvise, I've never kissed a woman without her knowing it was coming first.

And it dawns on me that if I want to seal the deal, I'll need to kiss a stranger.

My heart thumps against my ribs. My palms are sweaty. Her fake tears are causing an ache in my chest, and I don't like how it feels. Now I realize why I prefer action films. It's to avoid all this unnecessary heartache. Women crying has always been a weakness of mine. I want to spring into action.

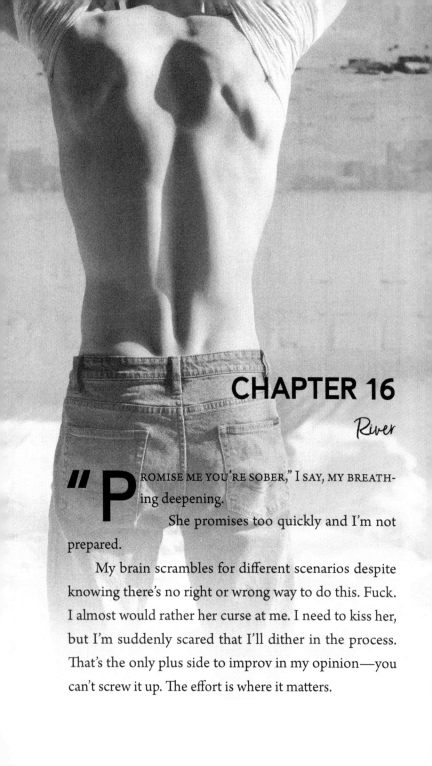

CHAPTER 16

River

"**P**ROMISE ME YOU'RE SOBER," I SAY, MY BREATHing deepening.

She promises too quickly and I'm not prepared.

My brain scrambles for different scenarios despite knowing there's no right or wrong way to do this. Fuck. I almost would rather her curse at me. I need to kiss her, but I'm suddenly scared that I'll dither in the process. That's the only plus side to improv in my opinion—you can't screw it up. The effort is where it matters.

"Look at me in the eye and say it. Tell me you're not lying."

Roxanne lifts her head and peers up at me. Our eyes meet. She blinks a few times, then says with a soft voice tinged with hope, "I'm as sober as the day we met."

Shaking my head, I'm unsure where to go with this now. Shit. She replies in the sweetest southern belle voice too, which I'm a sucker for.

I swallow thickly and lick my lips, thinking like a protective father who still loves the mother of his child whether he wants to or not. "Don't fuckin' lie to me. I can't take it."

She shakes her head frantically. Her chest rises and falls in short breaths. "I'm not. I promise. I'll do whatever you want me to do. I just want to see our daughter."

Something about her words cut into me. I'd never use her like that, like what she's offering between the words. Using women for my own pleasure doesn't get me off. To me it's the same as buying a blow-up doll. I don't need a "yes, daddy" girl. I need to know she wants what I want.

"I could never use you even if I wanted to. You're more to me than that."

"I'm not the same person I was when I left. I've changed."

The corners around her eyes soften with a yearning. She looks remorseful, and now I'm reading into this too much. My gut is telling me it's now or never, that if I don't kiss her already we're going to lose this.

"I'll do anything you want, be anything you need."

Roxanne swallows and stretches as high up as her tiptoes will take her. It's like she's inviting me. So I strike without a second thought, capturing her lips with mine. Her pillowy soft lips press effortlessly against mine and it causes me to pull her flush against my body. Roxanne tenses under my hold and I wonder if I've made a huge mistake now.

But then she kisses me back and I think I'm doing something right. Roxanne takes it a step further and slips her tongue into my mouth and doesn't wait for guidance. She kisses me at her own will. A burn spreads through my chest. It's consuming me in ways I've never felt before. I breathe into her and gently cup the sides of her face, kissing her back with the same intensity she brings to the scene.

"I've missed you. I never stopped loving you," she says, breaking the kiss, but there's something I don't like about it.

My brows crease. *This* doesn't feel sincere. I blink, reflecting on her actions. Roxanne changed the tone of her words and upped the rush in her touch.

A light goes off in my head, and it's the finale I need to bring us home.

I push her away and step back, hardening my gaze in her direction. Shaking my head, I say, "When it comes to you, I always get less than what you take. You'll do the same to our daughter if I let you. I don't want you getting her hopes up for nothing. You left once. I won't allow you to fool me twice."

Her eyes lower. The air around her turns cold. Roxanne strides up to me, and without hesitation slaps me across the face. I stand in complete shock. The room is still as we all wait to see what happens next.

"You son of a bitch. You know nothing. You can't keep her from me forever. She'll grow to hate you. Is that what you want?"

Can someone yell cut already? Jesus Christ.

Mustering up what I can, I try to think of something cruel to say. "If it saves her from the kind of pain you give, then yeah, I can handle the hate she gives. It won't last forever. It beats what's left over from you, that's for sure."

Emotions crawl up her cheeks. Tears fill her eyes. "Sometimes I wish I never laid eyes on you."

"Annnnd cut!"

My shoulders fall forward, and I let out a breath. Roxanne does the same and we share a smile with each other. There's commotion and low talking behind the tables. I can sense pairs of eyes on us, but we pay them no attention.

"Talk about the last thing I expected to happen," she says. Her eyes light up and it's almost as if they're smiling at me. "I tried not to slap you too hard."

My brows rise and I reflect on the audition. I can't stop the grin sliding up my face. She makes me giddy.

"I feel like I deserved it." I shake my head, surprised at how the audition unfolded. "I wasn't sure where we were going with that."

She laughs. "I guess that's the beauty of improv, right? Fully commit to the unknown."

I nod in agreement. Her effervescent eyes hook me. I don't even know what to call them. Hazel? The way she looks at me makes me feel like the only guy in the room. It's got me thinking I should apologize for the kiss now to be respectful, but I kind of don't want to. I got an excuse to kiss a beautiful stranger, and I took it.

The director walks around the table toward us. I stand up straighter. Roxanne notices and does the same. I see her swallow and watch as she brushes her hair behind her ear. He stands between us and clasps his hands together in front of his stomach. I don't get the sense he's not happy. I don't get the sense of anything at all.

"Thank you for coming at the last minute, Roxanne. If you can wait with the others in the sitting area, we'll let you know what your next step is." He pauses and we both seem to hold our breaths. "You both changed up the pace and it was refreshing to watch. Somewhat entertaining."

Roxanne frowns. She doesn't know she's the only one to have improvised, or that the room isn't filled with a bunch of anxious people now. I'd go as far as to say the director is pleased.

I rub the cheek she slapped and hesitate as I try to gauge her reaction. "I feel like I speak for the both of us when I say we . . . agree?"

Roxanne throws her palms up in surrender. She smiles and I see the director watch her closely the way I did. She's a sight to see up close. I bet she doesn't even know it.

"Figured if you got to kiss me, then I got to slap you. A hall pass, right?"

I blink, and stare at her. Did she just say what I was thinking just moments ago? Before I can stop myself, I ask her my next thought. "So you don't feel sorry for slapping me?"

She scoffs.

She actually scoffs, and it leaves me in an unusual state of admiration. Relief fills me with joy.

"No, not at all." Her head angles to the side as she reads my face. Sarcasm lights up her eyes. "Aww, you feel sorry for the smooching, don't you?"

My jaw drops. I can't believe my ears. "Only because I thought it was the respectful thing to do. Listen, I've never done this before." I shift on my feet awkwardly, yet the director hasn't moved. It's like he's taking notes in his head.

"Neither have I." She rolls her teeth over her bottle lip and bites down. She looks too damn cute for her own good. "I'm not a Delicate Debra. I can be Showcase Sally when I have to be."

The director laughs and turns on his heels. I find myself grinning too. "I'll catch you kids later. Wait outside, Roxanne. And tell your parents I said hello for me."

He struts off to talk to his people. I look over at Roxanne. "I don't know about you, but I think the audition went well."

She nods. "At least we got the first kiss out of the way, right?" She takes a step to leave and I feel my face falling. I don't want her to go. "See you around, handsome," she says.

I feel like I need to stop her.

I don't though.

I watch her walk out the door and get back to work.

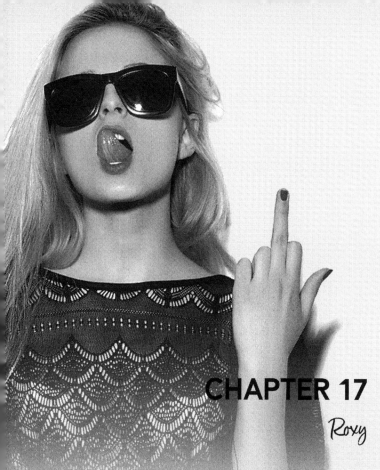

CHAPTER 17

Roxy

I WAIT WITH THE OTHER CALLBACKS, SITTING A FEW seats away from each other.

Rapid thoughts run circles in my mind and I try to remember if anything is amiss. The director was vague in the end. He seemed pleased enough to not ask for another scene, but he didn't state whether I moved on to the next phase or not.

Either way I can't wait to text Estelle to tell her what happened. Even if I don't get the part, the audition is one to remember.

My knee bounces anxiously as I sit and overthink, waiting to see what I'm supposed to do next. The audition replays in my head and I stress over alternate scenarios that could have played out. I bring my fingers to my lips. River's kiss was somewhat of a surprise. I'd thought for a split second he might kiss me, but then I wasn't sure.

And when he did, I welcomed it.

Who am I to say no to a kiss from a hot guy?

Stupid. I'd be stupid.

I was coming off the high from Brody when I was blessed with a kiss from another good-looking man. I had to take it. I figured if I wanted to sell the idea of us, then I would have to believe some aspect of it myself.

It was easy to do with a co-star like River. He exudes masculinity, and I'm a sucker for that. Deep down I revel in the thought of settling down with someone who can not only protect me and love me unconditionally, but also lift my ass up off the ground and fuck me against a wall like it's his God-given right. River seems like he could do that.

I forgot the camera was there and had lost myself to his sinful mouth. Holy, sweet Jesus, can the man kiss. The second River's tongue connected with mine, I lit up like the Fourth of July. He tasted like the soft peppermints my great-grandfather always had around the holidays. My eyes fell shut as our lips fused too seamlessly together and we gave each other to the scene. I wasn't thinking straight, and I gather he wasn't either, judging by the way he was breathing.

If that was his performance kiss, I can only imagine what he kisses like behind closed doors.

My stomach growls and brings me back to reality. I'm starving and could go for a hangover burger right now with sunny-side up eggs—

"Roxanne?"

I look over in the direction my name was called. My eyes widen. One of the studio executives is standing outside of the room I just came from. I didn't hear the door open because I was daydreaming about River.

"Yes?" I stand quickly to my feet.

"Your agent will be in touch with you." She looks at the others waiting in the chairs. "Callbacks, you're free to leave. Thank you for your time. Your agents will be in touch."

She turns away and disappears back into the room. My jaw slackens. I stand there, stumped. The others get up and walk away quietly.

My shoulders fall.

I guess this means I'm not a callback.

After I use the bathroom and splash some water on my face, I head downstairs and hope for better reception. I tried texting Estelle to see if she was around to pick me up, but the messages wouldn't deliver. L.A. has the shittiest connection for the amount of wealth in this town.

If she's busy, I'll just call our driver, but we have a thing where we call each other first. It comes naturally when you are best friends with your roommate.

I push the door open and step outside. The sun is blinding already. I put a hand up and look down the walkway for a shadow to stand under, wishing I had a pair of sunglasses. I try not to dwell on what just happened upstairs and lean against a red brick wall to call Estelle. My face twists at the stench in the air. The City of Angels smells more polluted than New York City.

My call goes straight to voice mail and I wonder if it's the connection again. I wait a few moments then walk near the building to see if it'll go through this time.

"It's my favorite girl," Estelle says. Her phone cuts in and out. "I'm kinda busy. Is everything okay?"

I smile. She sounds like she's in a hurry, so I say, "Yeah, everything is good. I finished my audition and wanted to see where you were before I called Dick."

Estelle and I hired a personal driver with the name Richard for the sole fact that we can legally call him Dick. I hear faint voices and splashes of water in the background. Sounds like she's near one of the hot springs.

"We're kinda in the San Bernardino Forest? Like deep in the forest. It would take me a few to get to you."

My brows shoot up, shocked to hear where she's at. I'm calling Dick after I hang up with her, but now I'm dying to know what happened after she dropped me off.

"I know I said I would pick you up—" Estelle

continues but I cut her off. Wind blows into the phone and it's hard to hear.

"It's no biggie. I'm more curious how you got over there and who you're with."

She proceeds to tell me it's the same guy from last night and some of his buddies, but she should be home in a couple of hours. There's a little commotion down the street that draws my attention. I look over my shoulder and notice it's the casting director. He's talking to a few men before he shakes hands and climbs into a car. My head tilts as I observe the scene.

"How'd the audition go?"

I grimace, unsure how to answer the question. "I thought it went well, but you know how Hollywood is." I pause and remember something my mom said often when I was a kid. "It's not who you know, it's who you blow."

"I don't like to suck dick unless I'm definitely getting something out of it."

She cracks me up. "Speaking of which, I need to call our agent and talk to him. If you can count on Von for anything, it's him being a snake. He'll find something out. I thought right then and there I was going to get a call-back, but I guess not."

"Nope. We're not having pessimism for breakfast. Call Von before you get an extra wrinkle in that fore-head of yours for nothing, then go home and take a siesta.

Later we're going to binge watch our favorite show while we gossip about our night and eat frozen pizza."

"You know the way to my heart." I joke. Another door slams behind me and I decide I need to get out of here before someone sees me. "Can't wait for our date later. I'm off to call our favorite dick and ask him for a ride."

Someone clears their throat behind me. My shoulders bunch and I cringe. I can't stand that sound. Turning around, I see River watching me with heavy eyes. He doesn't hold back. A blush crawls up my chest and I quickly end the call with Estelle.

One corner of my mouth pulls up. I slip my cell phone into my breast pocket and then wave with two fingers. River doesn't say anything, but I can see that he wants to. The enthusiasm sparkling from his eyes causes warmth to curl in my belly. He's inquisitive, and I like the way it feels.

I encourage him. "Go on. What did you hear?"

He's wearing a ballcap now and lifts it up to smooth back his hair. An adorable smile curls the corners of his lips. "The tail end of the conversation. You share a cock with someone?" My lips roll between my teeth and I press down to suppress a grin at how stupid it sounds. But I guess that's what inside jokes are. "Do I want to know?" He replaces his cap and threads his fingers behind his head. His shirt rises, and since I have no willpower at all for fine men, I blatantly look at the skin he's revealed.

I know he can see that I'm staring at him, but I look anyway, and I'm glad I did. The waist of his pants hangs low and allows me to see around his sides. River's not a lean guy. He's bulked up but broad with thighs that could crush me. A region of sandy golden curls dips past where the eye can see. Looks like the curtains match the rug.

A thought pops into my head. I look at River and see the satisfaction on his face.

"Take me for the best Bloody Mary and I'll tell you a story."

CHAPTER 18

River

SHE'S HARD TO SAY NO TO.

"Deal."

I say it before I can think. Even though I have a meeting in an hour with my agent, I decide he's going to have to wait. The truth is I need a break from work and the pressure of finding the perfect co-star. The studio is hell-bent on making this movie, insisting it will make millions of dollars and do all these wonderful things for people and careers, but only if the right actress is chosen.

She giggles. She almost seems shy. Her face lights up and I'm glad for not doing the right thing for once.

Roxanne's an easy diversion.

"Unfortunately, the best ones are made in my kitchen."

"Slick. You're slick." She nods her head at my game. I wasn't trying to take her home, but she made it too easy. "Where do you live?"

"Not too far from here . . . Santa Monica. Near the water."

Her head angles sharply and her brows crease slightly. "A bunch of fine men seem to live in that area. I'm thinking the Pacific Palisades isn't for me . . . Maybe I live in the wrong city."

Her comment kind of grates on my nerves a little bit. How many other *fine* men live there that she knows of?

"Is that where you share your cock?"

It blurts out from my lips. I realize how ridiculous that sounds and laughter gets the better part of me.

Roxanne nods her head, grinning from ear to ear. Her eyes are so bright they draw me in. "Yes, it is actually." She giggles harder. "We made a pact to never bring any other guys back to the house but Richard. Four years going strong, and Richard is still hanging in there."

Who the fuck is Richard?

"What makes your Bloody Mary better than the ones at every five-star restaurant on the corner?"

Roxanne jumps topics before I have a chance to process the first one. I'll figure out who Richard is later.

"For one, privacy. And two, I make it exactly how I want it to be made."

"What if I want bacon and shrimp in mine?"

"Thick cut or smoked applewood?"

"I only like the baby shrimp."

"Jumbo tastes like rubber."

"I want my shrimp seasoned with the taste of New Orleans."

"With more bacon on the side."

She raises one brow in appreciation. I step closer, liking where this is going. Her lips purse together and I feel mine doing the same.

"Olives soak in a floater," she says, then levels a serious stare at me. "I hate celery."

"Fuck the celery," I say.

Roxanne laughs and it feels like I'm on my way to home base. "My kinda man. Let's go before the traffic starts up. I'm starving and have a wicked hangover."

I lead the way and she steps next to me. Roxanne pulls out her cell phone and I catch a glimpse of it. Looks like she's texting a friend.

"You looked hungover up there," I tell her.

She pockets her phone and says, "I am. I got the call at the last minute. I wasn't home and threw on what I could and had a friend drop me off."

Explains the shirt. Figured it was her boyfriend's. "Do you need a ride home later?"

"No, thanks. I'll call Richard."

I frown. I have so many questions now but elect not to touch on them just yet. It's none of my business who this dick named Richard is anyway.

"I'm warning you now that I know my way around a kitchen," she says, and it takes me away from my thoughts.

"You like to cook?"

She turns her head in my direction and smiles. "I love it. I'm more excited to see your kitchen than having the drink now."

We get into my car and talk the whole way back to my place, mostly about food. Apparently, she has a secret talent no one knows about. She came alive over the topic and mentioned she had a custom-built kitchen installed when she bought her house she shares with a friend. She loves to cook savory foods but prefers to bake instead. Roxanne concocts recipes, and her friend Estelle tests them with her.

"You got plans tonight? I kind of want you to cook me dinner." My eyes widen at the realization of what I said. Immediately I correct myself. "I didn't mean it like that, you just make the food sound so good that my mouth is already watering. I'm hungry for something and I don't know what."

Roxanne gives me a sugary smile that makes my chest tighten. She turns in her seat and faces me. "I have a rule about cooking dinner. If I cook, then you have to do the dishes. You also have an obligation to bring the dessert."

I chuckle. Roxanne has a sweet tooth. "Fair enough. But what if I want to take you out?"

"Then I'll be your dessert."

I do a double take as I hear the words I've only ever fantasized about. She's unapologetic in her approach. Roxanne doesn't seem like she's kidding, so I push my luck to see where it takes me.

"Is that a yes for dinner tonight?"

She stares at me unblinking. Her mind is spinning with thoughts before a reluctant smile spreads across her face. "I guess it is." Roxanne shakes her head, happiness illuminating from her cheeks. I like the way it looks on her. "How did that even happen?" she asks in jest.

"I've learned not to question the good things that happen in my life but rather be thankful for them."

She sits back and I sense her relaxing into the bucket seats. "I like the sound of that."

It's not long before I turn down the cookie cutter streets to the one I call home. I can't stand the uniform look and rather something with a little more individuality, but it's convenient and I can't complain.

"Huh," I hear Roxanne say under her breath.

"What's that?"

She looks my way but turns back to the street only to watch the road with bewilderment. "Oh, it's nothing. Just thinking out loud."

"I do that all the time."

Pulling up the winding driveway, I'm relieved to see it empty. After days of traveling, I want to be alone for a bit. I put the car into park and turn off the ignition.

"Do you live alone?" Roxanne asks as I get out.

I shake my head and meet her around the front. Her eyes are everywhere, like she's painting a picture in her head. I've never been around a woman who evokes so many questions from me in a short period of time.

"Three roommates. Doesn't look like they're here though since the cars are gone."

"Don't tell me River Bolton lives in a fraternity house. I might have to bail on our date later."

I shake my head and chuckle. "These are guys I've grown up with my whole life. It's different with them. They're family." She watches too closely as I unlock the door. "Why are you staring at me like that?"

"Why do I feel like the world doesn't know who the real River Bolton is."

I push the door open, musing over her question. I go with the truth. "Because they don't. I prefer it that way."

Stepping inside, I throw my keys on the foyer table and glance around. I have no idea where any of the guys are, not that I care, but I'd rather be alone with Roxanne. The house doesn't look like it's in bad shape, just a few things amiss. I don't give two shits if the guys bring back women. Just stay out of my personal space and use protection. I ripped into them when I found a used condom on the floor once. Neither had owned up to it. I don't blame them, but fuck, respect your space.

I head toward the rooms we hang out in and notice there's a vacancy at my back. Turning around, I see Roxanne standing at the threshold. She's still outside, only she looks alarmed. My brows crease together.

"Do you need to be invited in?"

Her gaze snaps to mine. She blinks a few times like she's trying to regain her vision again. She points at the ground with her finger and asks, "You live here?"

"Yeah."

She's cautious and I don't understand why. I lift my nose to the air trying to catch a foul scent, but there's nothing.

"This is your house?" she confirms.

"Yes. I own this house." I shift on my feet and walk to where she's standing. "Are you okay? Is there something wrong?"

Maybe she's changed her mind. Wouldn't be the first time it's happened to me, and I'm sure it won't be the last. If Roxanne doesn't want to come in, I won't make her, but I don't want her to be frightened of me, which is how she's kind of looking right now. The last thing I need is my name splashed across the headlines again because a woman is nervous to be around me for no goddamn reason.

"We can go to a restaurant if you'd feel more comfortable." I stop. "Or I can take you home if your ride can't get here yet."

Doe eyes stare back at me. She shakes her head as she investigates my house from the doorway.

I'm really starting to feel like I don't know women at all.

"I think I'm in the twilight zone right now." Her brows

deepen. "How strange," she says under her breath. Roxanne pokes her head in further and peers around the corner. I glance over my shoulder in her direction toward the kitchen and billiards room, then I look back at her. She's lost in her thoughts but doesn't actually seem frightened like I thought she was before.

"Are you uncomfortable around me?"

Her brows deepen, but she meets me with an unwavering gaze. "If I were uncomfortable around you, then I wouldn't be here right now."

Relief settles through me. All my exes are crazy. I swear they've made me paranoid.

"I just had a moment of—"

"Déjà vu?" I answer for her before she can finish.

Roxanne side-eyes me and then nods slowly. "Something like that."

"At times I feel like living in Hollywood occasionally causes my reality to blend into the fantasies I've played. It gives the impression I've done this before."

She watches me carefully and agrees. Licking her lips, she steps inside and pulls out a smile that seems genuine, so I go with it. Her purse lands on the table, but she takes her phone with her. Roxanne is a little younger than the girls I usually hang out with, but she gives me a burst of energy I didn't know I was missing, and I like the way it feels. Which brings me to my next thought.

"How old are you really?"

"Old enough to buy alcohol legally."

She walks next to me. Roxanne has a flare about her that pulls on something deep inside of me. One half of me can control it. The other half can't.

"What is it with women lying about their age?"

"I don't have an issue hiding my age, but you're obviously older than me, so I figured I'd just answer the question burning in your eyes."

My brows lift. "Burning in my eyes?" More like a burning in my cock. She's beginning to fascinate me. "That's a new one."

"Yes," she says, giggling. And damn it, I like the way it hits me in the chest. I try my damnedest not to grin, but I fail. "I really am twenty-one, if that helps. Newly turned twenty-one. What about you?"

I rub the back of my neck. I'm old compared to her, but I try not to think about it. "Thirty-two."

Leading the way toward the kitchen, I'm eager for the Bloody Mary and what Roxanne is capable of in there. The way she spoke about food made me want to experience it with her.

I take the shortcut through the billiards room, and my gaze immediately falls on the pool table and the obvious spill it's taken.

Anger simmers beneath my skin. I live with a bunch of slobs. I'm getting sick of it. This isn't the first time we've made a mess in here, but we agreed not to tear it up after the last time. The closer I step I can already tell we're going to need to get the fabric replaced again. We had a high-top table put in the room to avoid this specific issue we keep having.

I stop and inspect the table closer. It's partially dried, and I'm forced to look around for the chalk that disintegrated into it.

It's clear that one of the idiots didn't follow the rules again.

Bending down, I rake my fingernail over the pasty white stain to see if it will come up. It flakes, and I flick over it again.

"Why do you only do action flicks?" Roxanne asks, sidling up to me. She purposely bumps her hip into me and causes me to stand up. She steps in front of me to bring my attention back to her.

Roxanne is good at what she does.

Whatever that is.

"Can't find a way to get the steam out, so you chase the bad guys and mount them into submission?" Roxanne leans against the table and stares up at me through her eye lashes. She says it in a way that's teasing and antagonistic.

A chill works down my spine. Women have a knack for calming men with their touch when a situation is heightened. She must've sensed my frustration and decided to cut into my thoughts with her voluptuous body, because my anger immediately fades when she invades my space and takes over.

I step closer and close the distance between us with my body. My cock has been hard since I felt the plush softness of hers in the audition. I've wanted to touch her again, but after the harassment I've dealt with over my ex, I'm much more reserved than I used to be.

"Rox," I say, briefly wondering where the nickname came from. Her eyes light up. I lean in closer to her mouth, but I don't touch her lips. "The only ones I mount into submission are the ones straddling my hips and raking their nails down my chest as they ride my cock into oblivion. There's usually tits bouncing in my face and an ass I'm smacking. That's the chase that makes the victory worth it." I pause when her innocent eyes stare up at me. "You might be too young to understand what that means though. Most kids your age fuck for fun, then move on to their next conquest just because they can. There's no satisfaction in that."

Roxanne purses her lips together. Rising on her toes, her breasts drag up my chest in a seductive manner. She isn't reserved like most females her age, and it hooks me in.

"Sounds like someone is getting hangry," she says. "Horny and angry." Damn it, I laugh.

The truth is I prefer action over other genres because it allows me to deal with my exes's harassment and constant legal battles we face. It's how I get my anger out. Fuck punching a bag or talking to a therapist.

But Roxanne doesn't need to know that.

A grin slides up my cheeks. I grab her hips and don't hold back. My fingertips press into her flesh. She softens under me and it allows her to feel just how horny she makes me. Her cheeks flush.

"Guess I'm not wrong," she says, her voice low. She grins up at me, and goose bumps work over my arms. "Must've hit a nerve though."

She sure fucking did.

And it makes me rock hard for her.

I could do one of a few things that quickly come to mind, but none of them promise a successful outcome except for getting her in the kitchen where she seems to be at home. I love to cook, but not the way she talks about it.

"Let's head to the kitchen and see what you're made of."

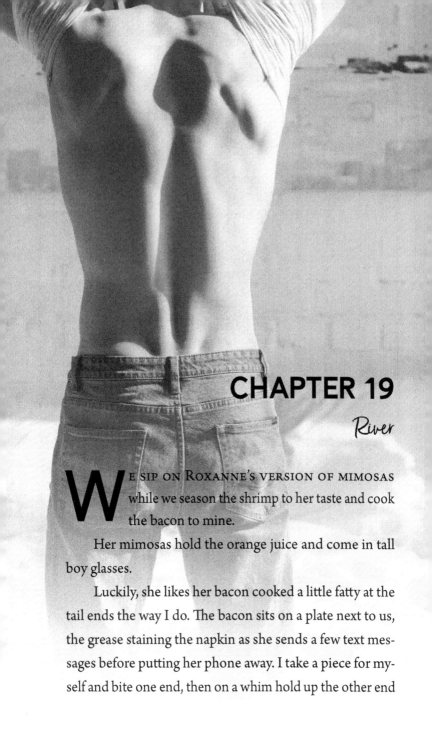

CHAPTER 19

River

WE SIP ON ROXANNE'S VERSION OF MIMOSAS while we season the shrimp to her taste and cook the bacon to mine.

Her mimosas hold the orange juice and come in tall boy glasses.

Luckily, she likes her bacon cooked a little fatty at the tail ends the way I do. The bacon sits on a plate next to us, the grease staining the napkin as she sends a few text messages before putting her phone away. I take a piece for myself and bite one end, then on a whim hold up the other end to her mouth. Roxanne leans in to bite it without looking. My gaze lowers. Her breasts fall into my view and I can't turn away as I stand holding my arm in the air. She bumps into me with her hip and then looks over at me with expectant eyes.

"Give me that," she says, then plucks the little piece I had left in my hand and tosses it into her mouth.

She licks her fingers and it sends a jolt of blood to my cock. I watch her tongue wipe the flavors clean. She wiggles her torso back and forth as she chews. Happiness blooms across her face. She looks too cute barefoot in my kitchen with just a shirt on.

I wonder if bacon is an aphrodisiac.

Stepping away, I walk to the cabinet and pull out two glasses. I think the prosecco is getting to me. I don't usually drink the stuff, but I'm feeling tipsy since we finished the bottle. We need to make the Bloody Marys. The pepper will straighten me up.

"Ready to make magic?"

"I already am." She pauses when I look over my shoulder and points to her face. "It's in my mouth."

Roxanne chuckles and brings the back of her hand to her mouth to stifle her laughter. It's stupid, silly, a bit immature, but I like it coming from her.

Her eyes light up, and she grabs the crystal from me, insisting the only way good food comes out of the kitchen starts with music. She puts on her favorite playlist and jumps into action.

We start making the Bloody Marys together. She dances around me as we cook. I try to offer help but ultimately give Roxanne the reins to let her do her thing. We bump into each other a few times. She flitters around the kitchen, and I can't deny that I like her presence. She's at home and the happiness shows in her face. It's not a side of her I've seen in the media.

"What the hell do you call this?" I say as I look at the outcome. I'm impressed.

"A meal supplement."

We toast, and I take a sip of the best Bloody Mary I've ever had. The taste erupts in my mouth and I look at her. I nod my appreciation, and she smiles around her straw. My gaze falls to her pouty lips. We stand there in silence drinking a few gulps together. I can't tear my eyes from her mouth as I suck down the drink too easily. I can't taste the vodka at all.

A song comes on and her face ignites with pure bliss. She sings the lyrics and holds the drink to her mouth like it's a microphone. Her voice is horrible, but she doesn't seem to care while she two-steps around me. I move to her tempo and bob in my stance. It's impossible not to. Roxanne is lost to her own world, and I kind of want to be there with her.

After the song is over, I clap my hands proudly. "Bravo," I tell her, beaming at her. "Bravo."

She curtsies and declares, "I'll be here all night."

It doesn't take much time to down the drink, just a few

songs. I could go for another one, but I have other things on my mind.

Mainly Roxanne.

"I'm not sorry for kissing you," I blurt out before I can stop myself. I'm not sorry and I feel compelled to tell her.

She carefully places her empty drink on the counter next to her and turns to me. "That's good because I wasn't looking for an apology."

Relief courses through me. I think there is a part of me that was hoping she'd say that. I want to feel her lips on mine again, and soon. She looks good enough to eat right now.

"I've never kissed a woman during an audition before," I admit, compelled once again. This time it's for personal reasons.

Her lips twitch behind her smirk. She nods, accepting my truth. "Why are you telling me this?"

I look down at the ice in my glass, then put it to the side. Roxanne meets my gaze, but I don't say anything. The air is tense between us as our eyes lock. I think about her question, but I don't answer it. I'm not sure how.

"You flirt when you drink."

I shrug. "Not really."

She shakes her head. "I'm not asking. I was telling you."

That's a first for me. "I don't think anyone's ever called me a flirt before."

"I find that hard to believe. Flirting comes in many forms. You're just more clever about it. More discreet."

I shrug again, unaware. "Maybe so."

Roxanne walks toward me on her tiptoes. She puts her arms around my shoulders and leans against my chest. I hold still, debating what to do next.

"What are you trying to say?" she asks, her soft voice raspy. She stares at my mouth waiting for an answer. It's hot the way she looks like she wants to take a bite out of me. "Because it sounds like you're trying to say that you want to kiss me again."

I hold her close and wrap my arms around the small of her back. There are so many things I want to say but keep my thoughts to myself. She's younger than me by more years than I anticipated, so I keep it aloof with her. Roxanne isn't good for my reputation, yet all I want to do is taste her lips again. I'm known to gravitate toward women closer to my age, if not older. They're more skilled and take sex seriously because their time is precious. I don't usually deal with youngins like Roxanne. Too much drama for one. And I like to make sure I get off when I get the chance. It's the only kind of release that lets me sleep at night.

"How about I help you out and make this easy," she says, urging me on. "It's probably a bad idea—"

"Then we need to do it."

Roxanne smiles. "See." She pokes her finger against my chest. "This is what I'm talking about. You're flirtatious. Probably even a little reckless." She pauses, slowing her words down. "A natural-born flirt is a danger to society."

"What can I say? It's more gratifying to watch my legs

swing over the ledge of a cliff than it is to sit in my house and hope the ambition I have will take me places one day."

Roxanne observes me, her hazel eyes pensive. "How is it you haven't matched with an actress for this film?"

I wince and pray she didn't notice. It's not something I want to talk about right now. "Guess they haven't found the right woman for me yet."

"Fair enough. Sounds like a bullshit answer, but I'll take it for now. Guess you and I are *risky business*."

I bark out a laugh over her cheesiness. Something about her here feels right. It could be the vodka warming my veins, but I don't question it. I feel at ease for the first time in months and not stressed about my next move.

"Tell me this bad idea of yours."

I like the way Roxanne's eyes twinkle. It makes me feel good. I already know I'm going to say yes. Subconsciously I think I needed her to take the first step and show me she wants me the way I think she does. My gaze roams her face and I exhale. She calms something inside of me and all it does is make me want more of it.

"You did cook us breakfast, it just happened to fit in a glass . . ." Her voice trails off, leaving the sentence open for me to interpret.

And I do.

"Are you telling me I can have you, right here, right now?"

My hands still on her waist.

My gaze locks on to hers.

"We can have each other," she corrects me. "Because I will be getting a piece of cake too."

She's steadfast. I search her face once more to see if there's any hidden meaning, but all I see is the green light in her eyes.

I make my move and strike with my lips. Roxanne meets my kiss immediately and thrusts her tongue into my mouth without hesitation. Our tongues collide and we both moan at the same time. Her skilled kiss takes me for a spin. A craving rushes down my spine. Gripping Roxanne's hips, I spin us around and shove her against the counter, plunging deeper into her mouth. Her body molds against mine too smoothly that I delve even deeper into her mouth. I want to taste every inch of her.

She meets me stroke for stroke and it only amps me up. Reaching down, I hoist her up onto the counter and place her down. Her back goes ramrod straight and the position shoves her breasts into me. Her ankles wrap around my back as I tackle her kiss, pulling her tongue around mine. I love when a woman locks herself to me. Makes my cock hard. I devour her taste, greedy for more. The kiss breaks and Roxanne gasps as I lean too far in.

"River!" Our movements are frantic. We reach out for the other when it dawns on both of us what's happening.

Embarrassment courses through me as I grab for her arm. I wasn't thinking straight when I lifted her and dug in like I was eating actual fucking dessert. I'm humiliated further that it happened with a woman eleven years younger.

She's hysterically laughing. I had Roxanne on the brain, and clearly nothing else when I placed her on the edge of my kitchen sink, and not the actual countertop. Her ass is too big, and she slipped back when I leaned in for more, dropping into the empty tub sink. No wonder she tightened her legs around me. She felt the drop coming before I could comprehend it. She can't stop laughing and it helps ease the shot to my ego.

I lift her out and pull her to me. She drops her legs to the floor and stands up. "I can't believe I just slipped into the sink." She chuckles and it comes from deep in her belly. "Oh, River." She laughs again, unable to control herself.

She reaches for my lips with hers, and surprise rocks into me that she's coming back for more. A flush works up my chest.

"I can't believe I let that happen."

"Must mean I taste *delicioso* then." She's pleased. And it makes me grin like a damn fool.

"If what just happened isn't example enough for how much I want you, then I don't know what is."

She slides her arms between our bodies so she can reach around and grip my ass. A growl vibrates deep in my chest as she tugs me against her. My cock strains toward her, and I know she can feel it. Roxanne is hungry like me.

"Talk about making a rookie mistake."

She giggles and it loosens the tension in my chest. "At least you didn't drop me, old man."

I rear back, grinning down at her. She's got my feelings

all out of whack and it makes me want to give her a giant bear hug. "Now I'm insulted. I'd never drop you."

I seize her hips and go back for more before she can utter more fucking nonsense.

Drop her. Who drops a woman? I knew what I was getting into the moment I took in the shape of her body. Kissing her mouth, I nibble on her bottom lip and tug it down with my teeth. I feel deprived, yet she's standing in front of me. I couldn't wait to dive into her plush softness and round curves, and now that I am, I act like I've never rubbed one out before. She's exactly what I thought she'd feel like and it has me wanting to be inside of her so badly.

"Tell me what you want," she says, breathing heavy. Her eyes look back and forth between mine.

The question causes me to pause. I've never had a woman ask me what I want during any kind of hookup, and it throws me off guard. The tips of her fingers dig into my ass cheeks, and it makes my dick jump. I like how low her fingers crawl to touch me. I look back and forth between her eyes. Fuck, I can't think straight with her hands on me, so I get right to the point.

"You got a body to die for and I want to take a bite of it. Right here, in my kitchen." Her eyes light up and I think she likes it. "It's been a fucking struggle and a half trying to keep my hands to myself as I watched you take over this space."

Roxanne lifts the hem of my shirt, and I reach behind my neck to pull it off for her. It drops to the floor in a soft heap. She takes me in with wide eyes and puts her hands on

166

my pecs before they trail down to my belt buckle. I've got a few old scars, but she pays no mind to them. Assertive fingers undo my pants. The zipper lowers and my cock is humming for release. Leaning in, she places a kiss to the center of my chest, then peers up at me as she pushes down my jeans. I step out of them. My erection is solid and I don't hide how she makes me feel. I want her to feel and see what she does to me.

"Next time don't hesitate, River Bolton. I'm enough to feed a family."

Next time.

A grin spills across my face. "Have you seen the size of me? I don't just come back for seconds," I tell her.

Her eyes flare. Roxanne reaches for the buttons of her shirt dress and slips it off. She drops it to the floor, then stands before me completely naked in all her glory, not shy one bit. Her confidence is powering.

"I feel like I'm in the twilight zone," I say, and track her collarbone with the pad of my finger. "How'd I get so lucky to have someone like you in front of me?"

She takes a deep breath and her chest rises. Goose bumps break out over her skin and I want to see it happen again.

I don't know what's come over me, but I drop to my knees and take her hips in my hold. Her fingers thread my hair and I lean into the center of her body, needing to taste her before I do anything. Without warning, I spread her pussy lips open and lick. Her knee jerks up and her heel kicks the cabinet.

"River. Oh . . . Wait . . . Oh, not . . ."

Her body jerks against me, and I hold her tighter while I flick the tip of my tongue on her nub. "Oh! Oh, hell on earth. This is so wrong, but it feels so fucking good."

She pulls my hair, trying to separate me from her clit, but she's no match for my tongue when it tastes good pussy. Her knees give out and she sinks to the floor, trying desperately to hold on to the edge of the counter with her elbows.

I maneuver her quickly to the floor and get back between her thighs. Roxanne shoves my face against her pussy before I can do so.

This is what I like.

"Lick my clit again. You're so good at it."

Her knees fall completely open. I stare down at her pussy thinking about how I could lick her all fucking day. She's spread out and I'm about to fest on her.

"Promise to come in my mouth and I'll eat you out better than anyone ever has."

She shakes her head, but her eyes are closed. Her pussy lips are already swollen and tender, and her cunt is dripping wet. Her hardened nipples catch my attention, and I notice how they're the same color as her pussy.

I bet if I gave her three good licks she'd melt in my mouth.

"No, I want to come when you're inside of me." Her hips lift and she groans, aching for me.

"You'll do both," I correct her.

"Okay."

She makes me laugh with how easily she agrees. With both my hands, I spread her pussy open and then pucker my lips around her clit. I suction the fuck out of it until she bucks against me. I'm relentless. I have this lustful passion roaring through me to feel her unravel between my lips. Her mound bumps into my teeth, but I don't stop. Roxanne moans my name and pulls her knees back to grant me more access.

The clit works every time. You just have to know what you're doing.

CHAPTER 20

River

PULLING UP TO SIT ON MY KNEES, I SCOOP ROXANNE'S ass into my palms and lift her off the floor to milk her for all she's got. She's exposed and at my mercy, it's a beautiful thing. Her hips tip back while I suck her pussy until she's withering in my arms and trying to escape. It's a sight to behold seeing her lost to the pleasure.

I heave her hips back and forth, drawing on her clit and rubbing the tender flesh with my tongue. I help her fuck my mouth as she thrusts against it. Her breathing deepens and she sighs in pleasure.

"River," she cries, changing up the speed to grind into my mouth. Her thighs jiggle and my cock thickens seeing her use me for her own pleasure.

She cups her tits and brings them together. She tugs on her nipples, twisting them to the point of pain. I can't wait to make my mark on them next.

"I want to ride your face," she cries out, panting hard. Her eyes are squeezed shut as she says, "Let me ride your face. You give good tongue. I want to sit on it."

My dick just shot off. I don't need to look to know I've got precum dripping from the tip of my pulsating cock.

I could marry her. I love a woman who knows what she wants.

"Don't have to ask me twice," I say, and we switch places easily. I lie back on the kitchen floor, suddenly grateful for the rugs. Before she kneels, Roxanne makes an obvious shift in her gaze and eyes my erection. My thighs spread and I reach between to stroke myself.

"Hmm." She smacks her lips in appreciation. Her nose twitches and I'm enthralled. "I'll be seeing you later," she says, talking to my dick.

I don't think I've ever spoken to my own dick before, but Roxanne just did.

She steps over my hips and gets on all fours. "Big mistake," I say, and grab one of her breasts to shove it in my mouth. I tongue her nipple and suck. I could choke on her breasts, they're so big.

"Goddamn you, River," she says, the pleasure unmistakable in her words. "Fuck."

Her tits are real and they're incredible to juggle. She collapses on her way to my mouth, her wet pussy wide open and leaking on to my stomach. An uncontrolled part of me awakens as her desire coats my naked skin. Roxanne doesn't embarrass and rubs herself on me. My cock strains and I change up the game, needing to be inside her already.

"You can't dangle these girls in front of me like that and not expect me to taste."

Her moan comes out raspy.

"Now you can get up here and fuck my face."

Roxanne climbs up my body. She straddles my throat and hovers her swollen pussy above my mouth.

"Good girl."

She looks tender as a steak. I open and she sinks down. My eyes close and I get lost in the joys of a woman's body.

"Oh, hell yes," she says against my mouth. "Flatten your tongue." I do and she rolls her hips down so her clit drags the way she wants it. Knowing where she's going and what she wants, I grip her hips and draw on her essence. Her back arches beautifully and the moan that leaves her lips makes my knees come up and squeeze my cock. The pressure is mounting between my hips just like it is for her.

My heart is racing as her hips thrust faster. A growl vibrates from my chest as she undulates on me like a wave of ecstasy bursts through her. I inhale her scent and become saturated by it. I can tell she's close and I thank my lucky stars because I can't hold on much longer for her.

I'm going to consume this woman.

Roxanne uses me to get off and it's a vision to see. She falls forward and braces herself on her elbows as she orgasms, lost to the sensations of pleasure. My fingers spread out as I cup her ass cheeks and hips. She's going to have crescent marks from the tension in her orgasm and the grip I have on her. I hope when Roxanne sees them later she remembers how my tongue penetrated her pussy at the tail end of her orgasm. I drink her slowly into oblivion.

"Jesus. How . . ." is all she can say.

I take great satisfaction in her response.

She falls forward in a heap, rolling on to her back. Her thighs are thick and full, her breasts like massive pitcher mounds I want to palm.

"Wow," she says, staring up at the skylight. "Thanks for the ride," she adds.

"I'm not done with you, Roxanne."

I spring into action and walk over to the drawer the guys and I keep plastic wrap and shit in. Pulling it open, I shuffle things around until I spot what I'm looking for.

Turning back to Roxanne, she's watching intently. "Did you just grab a condom out of that drawer?"

I look up from the questionable tone in her voice and nod.

"Why was it in there?" she asks. "Do you keep a bunch of them in there? Like a variety?"

I'm not sure myself now that I think about it. This just happens to be where we've kept them since we moved in. I shrug, puzzled.

"This is the stash drawer." I look at her as I try to explain this from a guy's perspective. There are several condoms in there. "It's like a lid for your cock, right?"

Roxanne stares, trying to suppress the thrill on her face. "That better be a normal condom or we're not bumping uglies."

For a second time I pause, my dick hanging out and all. I look over my shoulder, then back to Roxanne. I glance at my hands and flip over the foil. Am I missing something here?

A normal condom? My face twists up. What the fuck is that?

I flip the condom over and read it again, realizing that was why she looked at me the way she did and not over the fact that I was concerned about protection. Definitely not something I want to touch on right now, so I let it go and walk toward her since I got what I need.

"I'm not sure what the young kids use these days, but I like good old-fashioned lambskin."

I toss it on to her soft belly for approval. It lands near her belly button. My knees bend and I drop between her thighs. I roam her softness and like what I see. She has something for me to hold on to, and I can't wait. Roxanne reaches for the little square and brings it to her face. Is she really inspecting the damn condom?

"It's not expired," I tell her.

Waiting impatiently, I spread her thighs wide and massage my hands toward her pussy. I lean in and rake my eyes up her body. My cock is straining to take her already. The head is purple, it's screaming for release. She's going to feel like a warm blonde brownie once I get inside of her.

She finally hands me the condom.

"All clear?" I ask.

With a dreamy smile, Roxanne brings her arms above her head and stretches like a cat waiting for warm milk. She nods and drops her legs wide open for my viewing pleasure.

I've been with many women, few as content as Roxanne in her skin while at the mercy of a stranger. She's bared for me, and it brings out her sexy side she undoubtedly likes to be in, judging by the happiness painted on her face.

I want to take her higher.

"Just needed to make sure it's not ribbed for her pleasure or some hot and icy fancy one." She smiles wider. "The thinner the better. Nothing is like the real thing."

I tear the foil open and toss the wrapper to the side. "What's wrong with those? I thought your age loved them." Rolling the condom down my erection, I scoot closer on my knees. She side-eyes me at the nod I gave to her age and lets it go. I get the impression she's going to store it away for another time.

"Have you ever been on the highway and veered off to the side? You hit those little bumps and it wakes you up really quick? That's what ribbed is like. Speedlights that just never hit right." She almost sounds sexually frustrated and it works me up to a grin. "Those condoms are for people who are making up for what they lack in between their thighs when in fact we just want you to use what you got."

I palm my cock and aim it at her entrance. "Good thing I didn't grab that one. Do I want to know about the icy hot?" I say, probing her entrance. Her stomach dips and I do it again.

"I don't need a burning icebox in my vagina, thank you very much."

How she can make me chuckle right before I fuck her is fascinating. "At least we can agree on some things."

Taking the tip of my cock, I run it up and down her center, circling her clit a few times. She hisses between her teeth, her heavy lids allowing just a peek of green to show. I press into her dripping hole and insert the tip up to the crown. I take a deep breath. My jaw locks. She's already so warm.

"One thing you should know about me once I'm inside of you," I grit out. "I have one rule."

"What's that?"

"Let your body do the talking, not your mouth. Move with me."

Move with me.

Roxanne's breathing labors. She blinks a few times but nods. The tension between the back of my shoulders loosens. I want to focus on the orgasm and the pleasure it brings, not a conversation. We can talk later.

"Drop the dirty talk and fake moans. I understand the assignment. You better give me all you got, big guy."

I push another inch inside of her and my cock pulsates. Roxanne's hips tilt back to take me. If only she could see this view.

"Any last requests? I can't hold on another second."

She reaches her arms out for me. "Kiss me. If you want to keep my mouth shut, then kiss me."

Without another moment to waste, I watch as Roxanne's pussy stretches to take my cock as I push my way in all the way to the hilt. Her thighs press against mine and I lean over to take her mouth in one swift move. She tenses under me as I surge as far as her body will let me.

Experience tells me I've got a bigger dick than most men. That's not my ego talking but her quivering pussy that gives it away as she clenches around me. She gasps, her back bows, and she breaks the kiss. Her fingers thread my hair. Roxanne's nipples graze my chest as she grants me access to her neck. My lips meet her simple vanilla scent and my eyes roll shut.

"Shh . . ." I whisper. She nods, listening. "That's a good girl."

My chest tightens. Something about calling her a good girl sends a rush of blood to my cock. I'm acutely aware that I like the fact that she's younger than me despite not looking like it. She's built bigger than females her age in Hollywood, so I don't have to worry about pounding into her. I can take her how I want. That doesn't happen often, and it gets me geared up thinking about how good the orgasm is going to taste.

"Just give it a second to adjust," I say, slowly rocking into her. Despite her stiffness, I haven't stopped working her pussy. "Uncoil your hips and open up to me." I cage her in with my arms and capture her lips. I realize she might not be used to having a man fuck the pleasure right out of her. I lighten up a little but not by much, and feel her body become pliant under mine.

As I look into her eyes, she's about to see just how wrong the media can portray someone. I'm a lover, not a fighter. I'm nothing like the characters I've played. I'd rather make war between the sheets than on the streets.

I'm not as charismatic on the inside as I am on the outside. Yet her hands are all over my body like she can't stop touching me. I take her for granted and pump into her as she pulls on the skin on my back. A groan deep in my chest vibrates around our kiss. My teeth gnash into hers. I want more of her. Being in a woman's body is the best part of my day.

I strike her clit a few times and her breathing peaks. Roxanne doesn't shy away and surges into my thrusts one by one. An orgasm prickles the back of my legs and it moves fast. My toes curl and my knees scrape into the rug as I plunge into her soaking pussy. Her teeth gnash into mine and it only makes me crave her more. We're like two rabid animals fucking on the kitchen floor.

Our hips buck unapologetically to get what they want

from the other. I lock my knees straight and heave into Roxanne's pussy knowing she's about to tip over the edge. She twines around my body and uses it as leverage to take her higher. We hold on as an orgasm wracks through the both of us. I come harder than I ever have and unload into the condom. I shove her hips against mine and move into them, making sure I hit all her depths. The sex is so good even I'm making little sounds and huffing hard like she is.

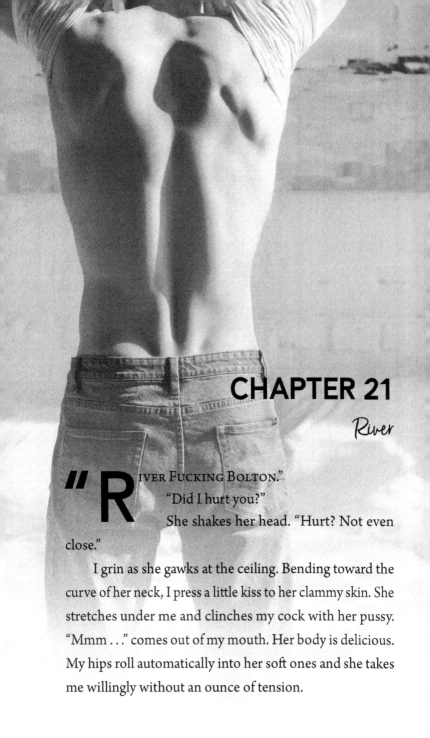

CHAPTER 21

River

"**R**iver Fucking Bolton."

"Did I hurt you?"

She shakes her head. "Hurt? Not even close."

I grin as she gawks at the ceiling. Bending toward the curve of her neck, I press a little kiss to her clammy skin. She stretches under me and clinches my cock with her pussy. "Mmm . . ." comes out of my mouth. Her body is delicious. My hips roll automatically into her soft ones and she takes me willingly without an ounce of tension.

"Who knew?" she says. It almost sounds like a giggle. "I think I'm delirious. I can't believe I came so fast like that."

"Damn, woman. I can't tell if I should be insulted or not."

Her ruby cheeks bring out her giddiness. I like the sound on her. "Trying not to make a sound was oddly erotic. It made the sex a thrill, like we were going to get caught or something. I got really wet just hearing our bodies."

I pepper kisses over her jaw until I reach her mouth, wondering where she's been hiding all this time. "You are the definition of a lazy Sunday morning."

Rearing back, I sit on my knees and carefully pull out of her. The condom comes out clear with nothing more than her pleasure dripping from it. I grin inwardly, thrilled it wasn't tinged with pink for once. A glance between her puffy, reddened thighs tells me I need to grab her a washcloth. But seeing her skin turn colors from the sex we had only entices me to stay there.

I stand up and roll the condom off my semi-hard dick and toss it to the garbage. She's spread out like a butterfly. She hasn't moved and I like that. Tells me she's sated. I'm ready to go at it again with Roxanne but decide that since I'm going to have her tonight the wait will be worth it.

I grab a paper towel and run it under the water, wondering how the hell this day turned around. I was dreading the next phase of auditions until she walked in and changed everything.

Turning around, I hand it to her.

"Can you open the freezer door for me, please?" she asks.

The space between my brows crease. The freezer?

I nod. Maybe she's hungry. We only had a few pieces of bacon and shrimp. The older I get, the less I understand women and their needs. Sometimes I find it's better not to ask questions and just do what's asked.

"I got you."

I watch as Roxanne scoots back to aim her body toward my refrigerator we just had sex by. I pull the side door open, and she brings her knees up and drops them back. A dreamy smile fills her face as the freezer air falls over her naked body.

"Ahh."

My head tilts to the side. "Are you . . ."

"Cooling myself off? I am," she states.

I look around for where my shirt ended up. Roxanne finishes wiping off her inner thighs, then hands me the paper towel. I take it and toss it in the trash next to the condom. I watch as she toes the freezer door shut but doesn't move.

"I'm going to need to soak with a bath bomb after this. By the way, I love Wagyu beef."

Shaking my head, I pick up my pants and pull them on, forgoing the boxers. "Stalking my goods?"

Her gaze drops to my dick, then she meets my eyes again. Her blatant joy makes me feel lighter inside. Her innocence prevails, but it doesn't bother me like it normally would.

"Maybe," she says, and waits a beat. Then she sits up and blurts out, "I have a recipe that will knock your socks off. The meat melts in your mouth."

Roxanne's eyes are wide and her face lights up as she speaks with her hands. She makes me feel like I've known her for ages. Crossing my arms over my chest, I lean against the counter and watch her with amusement. What puzzles me most is how at ease she is sitting cross-legged in a kitchen that's not hers while totally buck naked.

She rouses a side of me I'm not familiar with. I stare at her, wondering where her vibrance comes from. It's strong enough to awaken the curiosity in me. Where her sense of liberation comes from makes me want a taste of it.

"What? Why are you looking at me like that?"

I frown, realizing I've been lost in my thoughts. I let it go when I see the way she's looking at me. This whole situation is comical with her here on my floor. I'm trying not to question my luck again, but I'm having one of the best days I've had in a long time, and I want to make it happen again.

I laugh under my breath as I wonder where these fucked-up thoughts are coming from.

"You're talking about frozen beef, but all I see is the rack I want sitting in front of me." She glances down at her breasts, then smiles up at me.

"Does that mean I can make it for you tonight?" she asks, pleased. My gaze roams her flushed face and wild blond mane. My chest tightens as I stare into her hopeful eyes. I want to give her what she wants.

I shrug and push off the counter, then offer a hand to help her up and bring her to me. Her breasts press against my chest. I savor the touch of her nipples grazing mine, and I wrap an arm around her back and one lower so I can grab a chunk of her ass. She throws her arms around my shoulders and stands on the tips of her toes to reach me.

"I've never had a woman cook for me."

She's aghast. Slightly mocking, but more surprised than anything.

"Not once?" she asks, and I shake my head.

"How is that possible in your stone age? All those years and not one?"

I smack her ass and palm it lightly to feel it shake against me. I prefer a thicker woman, like the one in my arms. A low vibration escapes my throat. She knows what she did because she follows it up with a giggle and wiggles her hips to taunt me. My eyes lower and adrenaline spills though me.

"You can cook whatever you want, or I can take you out. Either way, I'm taking a bite of this tonight." I give her ass cheek a good squeeze.

"Yes, sir!" She jokes.

Before I can think better of it, I press a kiss to her smiling lips. Roxanne responds all too well. Blood rushes to my cock as I fist her hair and smush her face to mine, kissing her deeply. I spin her around and press her against the counter, thrusting my tongue in her mouth. She hikes her knee up around my hip. I wedge a thigh between her legs and bump it against her pussy. There's an unfilled need residing in me only Roxanne has ever touched on, and it's turning me into some kind of fiend for her.

"You're not like the others." I pant into her mouth.

"What does that mean?"

I shake my head. "I don't know. You're just . . . different."

"I'll take that as a compliment."

"Good. Because it is."

Before I lean in to take her lips again, I tell her what's on my mind. "I'm looking forward to tonight with you."

This time I kiss her much slower and it's almost too good. I'm making out with a woman much younger than me, and it's got my dick rock-hard and wishing the kiss never ends.

Roxanne's a needy girl. I can tell she wants my cock again by the way she's riding my thigh, and I want to give it to her. My tongue delves deeper into her mouth and we kiss passionately.

"I should get going," she says, breaking the kiss all too soon.

I groan in protest but agree when I hear the faint sound of loud music coming up the driveway. I look behind my shoulder to locate Roxanne's shirt dress. Being with her made me completely forget I live with three other men who could show up at any minute. The last thing I want is anyone to see her naked body. I'm not a fan of putting my woman on display for others to ogle. She's mine. I don't do the whole look but don't touch crap. Just don't look and we'll be cool. The guys know that, but I don't chance it anyway.

I pick up Roxanne's shirt and hand it to her. She turns it right side out and then slips it over her arms. I watch as she buttons up the goodies. A door slams outside, and I turn in the direction of the sound. I can't tell if it's a neighbor or not.

"Thanks for the rendezvous," she says softly, then gives me a little peck.

"That sounds better than a one-night stand."

"That's why I said it. Do you care if I grab a water?" she says, and I nod toward the fridge with my chin. She walks to it as the front door opens. It slams with a heavy clunk.

Roxanne looks at me as she uncaps the water bottle. She takes a sip. "Who did you say lives with you?"

Before I can respond, the footsteps grow closer and I look to see who's here. It's been a few weeks since I've seen the guys, so I'm not sure what they're up to.

"Yo!" I hear, and it echoes through the walls. "Is that you?"

A smile slowly spreads across my face in anticipation. "In here."

Roxanne mouths, "Who?" But I don't have the chance to respond.

My face lights up as I see who rounds the corner.

"Brother, it's good to see you."

CHAPTER 22

Roxy

MY EYES NEARLY POP OUT OF MY HEAD. I DON'T blink in fear I might miss something.

My jaw drops.

It flat out falls open and I thank God River doesn't see.

I'm speechless and watch as River walks over to Brody and gives him a bear hug.

Brothers!

Brody observes me over River's shoulder, penetrating me with his stare. The same Brody who gave me multiple orgasms. The same Brody who I had mind-altering sex with last night.

My eyes shift frantically between them. When did River get a brother, and why has no one heard of him?

I shoot a fleeting glance at Brody and grip the water bottle tightly in my hands. Is he going to say something to his brother? Or keep our night of hot sex a secret?

I groan inwardly.

Oh, I'm definitely going to hell for this little escapade. I clench my eyes shut and wonder how I got myself into this mess. Estelle is going to have a field day. This is borderline incest.

I feel lost, unsure whether I should tell River what I did with his brother last night or keep it a secret. I can't help that it happened. But now that I think about it, it does sound like I floozied it up to tag team both brothers in one night.

Dear God. What is wrong with me?

Okay. I did floozy it up, but that's who I am. I like sex. No, scratch that. I love sex. And when I'm touched just right, it's all I can see, it's all I want. I had zero plans to have sex again so soon, but once River put his hands on me, that was it. His touch is just as enticing as his brother's.

"Did you say brother?" I ask to make sure I'm not panicking for nothing. River nods and I can't believe my odds. "I didn't know you had a brother."

My stomach twists and my heart pounds in my chest. I don't know what to say. I don't know what to do. I'm looking at River, but I can feel Brody's stare on me, and it's taking everything in me not to look in his direction.

"Most people don't. This is Brody. He's one of the guys who lives with me. Brody, this is—"

"Roxanne Bardot," Brody says.

I freeze up, my eyes go wide. My cheeks redden. I don't know whether to say I know him or not. And if I do, should I add that I had sex on their pool table?

Mother of all gods.

The pool table.

I almost went into cardiac arrest when River flicked the dried up remnants with his nail.

That's how I knew I was at the same place, but still I had doubts in the back of my mind. I had been too worked up last night to register where I was or even care. I should have cared, but my mind had only one focus at the time. Brody.

"You guys know each other?" River asks, brows creased.

"Everyone knows who Roxanne is," Brody says quickly, his hypnotic eyes pulling me in.

His stare cuts through me. It's just like when our gazes locked for the first time at the Sunset Den. How can I be attracted to two brothers who are vastly different?

Before I send myself into a tailspin, I thrust my hand out to introduce myself. I swallow thickly and hope Brody goes along with it. It's the only control I have left of the situation until I can figure out my next step. I don't want to come between two brothers.

I have no choice but to give my best charming smile. Brody's palm slides against mine and I pray for the best.

"It's a pleasure to meet you," I say automatically.

A shadow crosses Brody's pensive eyes. The moment the words leave my lips I regret them. Guilt slams into me instantly. I know I've made a mistake. I wish I could take it back, but it's too late. Seconds pass, but it feels like minutes. It's like improv all over again.

"The pleasure is all mine," Brody says, going along with my ruse.

My stomach drops. River backhands Brody in his shoulder and it breaks our contact. "Hey now," River says. "It's good to see you. I wasn't sure when I was going to."

I sigh inwardly and we drop hands. I don't miss the possessive pitch in River's playful words and it makes my breathing more uneven. Brody rakes a heady gaze over his shirt I'm wearing. I wonder if he's thinking about our time together and the things he made me experience.

Heat prickles the back of my neck. The awkwardness is on a level ten out of five, but River doesn't seem to notice. I watch them speak to each other and exchange questions. Hollywood is touch and go, so people are hardly here for long stretches of time. I give them a few minutes while I text Estelle an SOS and send her my location.

"Do you want a Bloody Mary? We just made them," I hear River say. "Fair warning, you might get drunk."

River walks around me toward the stove while Brody takes in my disheveled hair and the buttons that don't match up. He knows what I look like freshly fucked, and this is it. A friction fills the room that leaves my stomach feeling uneasy. His eyes eat me up when his brother isn't looking, and I kind of like it.

"Sounds fun to me," Brody says, then glances at his brother. He takes a step in my direction and my breath hitches in my throat. I wait for his next move. His scent invades my senses and I feel it wash over me. I don't think he has any idea how potent he is. "I'll take one before I wash off last night. And this morning."

"One of those kinds of nights, huh?"

I hear the grin in River's voice like he knows exactly what Brody is talking about. I want to ask, but I don't. The less I interact the better.

"Oh yeah. Like the good old days."

River laughs. "Nice. I haven't had one of those in a while."

My lips part and I hope they stop talking. Brody smirks and my jaw bobs subtly. River has no idea that his answers are causing mad sexual tension between me and his brother. Brody is getting a kick out of it. His provoking is nothing more than enticement that makes my heart pound.

"It was alright." He pauses, and before Brody says it, I know where he's going. "She was kinda messy."

My eyes lower. I narrow my gaze at him, roused. "Scumbag," I mouth at him.

Game on, broski.

"Roxanne?" River asks. "You want another too, right?"

"Definitely. Hold the tomato juice this time."

He chuckles under his breath. I hear commotion behind me as River gets out some glasses. River's talking, but no one is listening. Brody is entertaining him, but he isn't paying attention either.

With his brother not watching, Brody discreetly slides his palm under my shirt and cops a feel of my bare ass. My eyes widen as he brings a finger to his mouth to shush me. He leans in and bites my neck and grabs a breast at the same time. I stifle my gasp as he quickly moves his fingers to my pussy.

He shushes me again as his fingers glide over the inside of my thigh. His brazen actions cause my brows to shoot up. My eyes widen as he touches me where his brother's mouth has just been. A delectable smirk curls the corners of his lips when he touches me. Warmth seeps from my pussy and my hips yearn for more. I grind against him.

Of all the fucked-up sexual situations I've found myself in, this debacle is a challenge I never saw coming. Brody's a snake behind his brother's back.

"So, you do have leftovers," he whispers low enough so only I hear it. His eyes lower and I bite the side of my lip. He notices. "Thought so."

Brody presses his hips to mine and rocks into me. My heart drops into my gut as desire rips through me.

I hate that I want him again.

I'm worried River will see us, but Brody is swift and

steps away, walking toward him. He pats River on the back but looks over his shoulder at me, leaving me breathless.

Brody wanted me to feel his erection.

"Where's your shirt?" Brody asks.

River laughs at his question and counters him. "Where'd you just come from?"

Brody leans on the marble island with his elbows. He's looking at me while his brother's back is to us. I pull out the olives and eat them all in one shot. I need to get the hell out of here.

"I got inspired and went to my studio. Spent a few hours there."

River gives him a fleeting look. Brody's on the mark and looks at him before he can catch on to anything.

"Yeah? When was the last time you were there? Paint anything good?"

I wrack my brain trying to remember if Brody mentioned his art but nothing comes to mind. "What do you paint?" I ask curiously.

I immediately regret the words. Fuck. I need to think before I speak. He's all too eager to answer.

"Naked women."

My heart is thumping in my throat. Brody likes to play dirty. And as much as I hate to admit it, so do I.

"Naked women?" I repeat. "No couples? No men?"

"Only a woman's body can evoke a deep enough emotion to influence with paint. You'd be surprised of the clientele who want authentic painted women in their house. There's a large demand."

My eyes narrow at him. "What do you mean when you say authentic? What else would it be?"

This time River chimes in. "He uses real models when he paints. They pose for him."

I glance back at Brody. Jealousy curls at my ends and I don't like it.

"Naked? She just lies on a couch like Kate did when Leonardo painted her in the *Titanic*?"

They both laugh and the sound is nearly distinguishably the same tenor. I look back and forth between them. It's the only visualization I have to go on.

The things one learns growing up on location sets in Hollywood.

Brody's light chuckle eases me. His gaze is sincere and my shoulders relax. "It's not always like that, but yeah, she poses how I want her in a location I set up."

"Do you know these women personally? Or do you put an ad out?"

"Some are from word of mouth." He pauses and I feel like I won't like his next words. "Some are lovers."

A chill runs down my spine. I need this vodka to kick in ASAP.

"Did you have a woman at your studio this morning?"

A smirk splays behind his beard. This could go one of two ways.

"Not this time. I used my imagination."

"You're covered in paint," River says. "Where'd your inspiration come from?"

My gaze drops to his black shirt that's splattered with vibrant pastels of greens and yellows. I thought it was the style of the shirt and paid no mind to it, but I was wrong.

He grins at his brother and it's kind of sweet. "You know I never kiss and tell."

River looks at me. "Brody markets his paintings with confidentiality. No one knows whose body it is. He won't tell a soul. Not even me."

In some way, knowing that relieves me. But it also makes me wonder what the hell he painted this morning.

River asks, "Gonna see her again?"

"I see her right now," Brody says, and taps near his temple. They clink glasses and toast.

I look back and forth at both and wonder how I didn't see the connection. They have the same identical colored eyes and little dimples on their cheeks but on opposite sides. Even their hair color is the same. I'm so stupid. This is what I get for being under the influence of alcohol and good dick. Their smiles are too in sync. The way they look at each other with knowing eyes yet look so different makes me wonder something.

"How many other brothers do you have? Who else lives here?" I ask. "Any other family in showbiz I'm not aware of?"

"Two aspiring actors live here, Talon and Kenneth. No other family in the business."

Relief washes through me. I was worried I may have had sex with one of their relatives and didn't know it. Those two names don't ring a bell, but if I see their faces, it might.

"Who's older of the two of you?"

"I'm older by sixty seconds," River says proudly.

My brows fuse together as I glance down at what's left in the glass, bemused by his response. *Sixty seconds?*

Then it hits me.

Twins.

Instantly I look to Brody. I already know what he's going to say.

"River and I are twins."

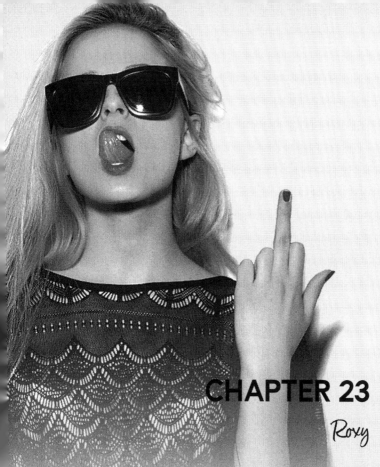

CHAPTER 23

Roxy

"**T**WINS?" I BLINK, STUNNED. "BUT YOU LOOK nothing alike."

I groan inwardly. What a stupid response. I know there's more than one type of twins.

"We're fraternal," Brody adds.

I'm at a loss for words. Not only brothers, but fraternal twins.

I stare wide-eyed and unblinking. They're twins who can't look more opposite yet they're so alike.

Thank God River wanted to use a condom.

I'm a certified brother fucker.

Wait until Estelle hears about this. She's never going to let me live it down.

"That's the look we usually get," River says, nodding with his chin in my direction. My eyes scrutinize them in astonishment.

I laugh it off and put on a façade to not draw any unwanted attention. I push back a lock of hair that's fallen over my cheek. Heat climbs my chest and blossoms through me.

"Yeah, I wasn't expecting that. It's kind of interesting to see and be in the same room watching you guys."

"We get that often too."

A cell phone rings, and I sigh with sheer relief. Saved by the bell . . . Well, er, cell phone. It's not mine, which reminds me I need to check if Estelle is on her way. I glance around as River picks up his cell. My heart is racing and my fingers are tingly as I scan my messages. Nothing from my agent, but one from my bestie.

You're never going to believe what the fuck happened, I text her.

She responds immediately. *Give me a hint before I crash and die and miss out on this great news.*

I blink and wonder about the kind of gossip I want to drop on her, then I decide to just go with it. She'll help me deal with it when she gets here.

I'm a brother fucker.

There's a pause before her messages come in a cacoph-onous harmony.

Bitch.
I am on the
motherfuckin
way

Knowing she's on the way, I place my drink in the sink and listen to River. He looks at me and I get the hint. He pulls the cell phone away from his face and whispers, "Give me a minute, this is the director."

This is my cue. Shaking my head, I mouth for him not to worry and that I'm going to go. I hitch my thumb over my shoulder and he walks around the island back to where I stand. River cups the back of my neck and places a kiss to my forehead. "I'll see you tonight," he says before he's strid-ing toward another room.

My heart thumps in my chest as River disappears. I don't look at Brody, but I can feel his gaze burning into me. He hasn't moved. He's waiting for me.

I roll my bottom lip between my teeth. A door clicks shut, and I know I'm completely alone with Brody.

I turn to look at him and hold my breath.

Brody pounces.

"Was I not enough for you?" he asks, his voice low as he nestles up to me. "Because the stain on my pool table says otherwise."

My eyes roll shut in embarrassment. Brody was incredible. Definitely not a one-hit wonder.

"River thinks one of the guys spilled a drink."

The corners of his lips curl up and it sends a zing to my clit. "Is that what we're going with?" he asks, and I nod, unable to answer over the beating my heart is taking right now.

"I hate lying," I tell him. I wish I hadn't, but at the same time maybe it was better that I did.

"So do we," Brody says, answering for him and his brother.

Inhaling a deep breath, my hands find his forearms to resist his closeness. It's making my thoughts hazy again. Except I don't push him away like I thought I would. My fingers curl around the material of his shirt and I fist it, pulling him closer. He hums out a low vibration and entraps me.

Brody's erection is thick and hot against my thigh. Heat washes over me as I think back to when he was inside of me and how he took care of me after. How he couldn't keep his hands to himself. How gorgeous his cock is without any barrier. The colors on his chest have me more curious than ever now knowing he's an artist. An artist is particular about what is inked on to their skin forever.

"I should leave. My ride will be here soon."

"How convenient."

Silence fills the air. His lips are so close to mine that they're almost begging for me to taste them.

I look into Brody's eyes. Guilt slams into me again. He's like a rip current, and I'm stuck in the path trying to swim against it. He pins my hips with his and then cups my cheeks, forcing me too peer up at him.

"Did he use protection when he fucked you?" I don't respond, but he can tell the answer by the way I look into his eyes. He's thrilled. "Doesn't surprise me. In case you weren't aware, River follows the rules."

I blink. "And you don't?"

He huffs out a sour laugh, and says, "He doesn't like to share with me."

Brody kisses me, slowly, deeply, passionately, giving me his tongue and owning my mouth. His strong hand remains protectively over my throat. It warms my blood and causes my pussy to wet my thighs. My arms circle his backside as my fingers search to touch every inch of his body.

"Was I not enough for you?" he asks once more, breaking the kiss. "Even after I licked your pussy goodbye, you wanted more? I left you hanging so bad you had to go fuck my brother? If you wanted something else, all you had to do was ask."

My chest rises and falls, my breathing erratic. "I didn't know he was your brother."

"You're missing the point, Rox."

His palm shifts with my throat when I swallow. Brody notices and rubs the pad of his thumb over the skin.

"I wasn't looking for anything else when it happened," I say softly. It's the truth.

Brody is a savage kisser. He slams his mouth over mine once again and draws out a breathless kiss from me. His cock digs into my hip and I wiggle against my own will. I try not to hold on to him, but I can't help it. I want more. My heart is pounding against my ribs to stop this, but the warmth of his body pulls me closer. Being in Brody's arms makes me forget the world and my problems.

I think about his question, torn on how I should answer. There's no right way to answer, but one thing I do know is that I won't start lying to both brothers.

Breaking the kiss, I look Brody in the eyes. He stares at me with his soul and I hate that I can feel it. I don't want to hurt him, but I have to tell him the truth.

"You were more than enough for me," I admit honestly. "But so was your brother."

Brody shoves himself away for me, scowling at my words. I wipe my mouth with the back of my hand and wonder if I should have left that last part out.

My phone dings, and I know it's Estelle without looking. Another text comes in. I bet she's around the corner. Brody doesn't say anything, and I don't blame him. I wouldn't know how to take it myself.

I decide to see myself out. Stepping away from the sink, I eye a bottle of prosecco untouched sitting on the counter. I'm going to need that.

I swipe it as I pull out my cell phone and walk toward the billiards room. Brody stops me with a light hold on my wrist. I grip the foil on the neck of the bottle and muster up all the willpower I have left to turn to look at him.

Brody's thumb rubs small circles on the inside of my wrist.

"I guess I'll be seeing you tonight," he says, his voice enticing.

He grins, but I give it right back. It's not over until the fat lady sings. My phone dings again. Any minute Estelle's going to honk the horn if I don't hurry up.

Leaning up on my toes, I press a kiss to his stubbled cheek and make my way toward his mouth. I give him a light kiss. He pauses and then kisses me back harder.

"You're forgetting one thing, playboy."

"What's that?"

I smile, knowing I won this round. He's not going to like my next set of words. They're going to taunt him, and I relish in delight knowing that.

"I'm not yours tonight." I bite his bottom lip. "I'm his."

To be continued

ACKNOWLEDGEMENTS

Thank you to the wonderful women who helped make this spicy shorty possible. Writing a book is not a one-person job. It takes a team to bring a vision to life and without these incredible angles in disguise, I don't think I would be writing this right now.

Tasha, Jessica, Victoria, Matti, Samantha, each of you bring something completely different to the table. I truly love how we uniquely blend. Your love for this story and the support you've shown is what gave me the courage to take a chance with words again. I am forever indebted to you. It's been a journey back from hell and I cannot thank you enough for guiding me to the light.

Thank you to my crazy sister. You're my biggest cheerleader and inspire me more times than I can count. I have so much fun plotting books with you. I still can't believe we're besties and talk on the phone all day long after how much we couldn't stand each other growing up.

To my husband who understood the need to neglect life for a bit so I can write this book, thank you for not complaining about the insane number of hours I work. You saw I was finally writing again after all the turmoil and quietly stepped in so I could focus. That made a world of difference and mattered so much to me. I'm working on not working fourteen-hour days.

You're Mine Tonight was a personal challenge for me, one I was determined to see through to the end. Roxy, Brody and River gave me the freedom to write romance the way I like—unapologetic and spicy—and the chance to bring a world to life that's been marinating in my head for a while now. I can't wait to take you on a ride with *We Own Tonight*.

ABOUT LUCIA FRANCO

Lucia Franco resides in sunny South Florida with her husband, two boys, and two adorable dogs that follow her everywhere. She was a competitive athlete for over ten years—a gymnast and cheerleader—which heavily inspired the Off Balance series.

Her novel *Hush, Hush* was a finalist in the 2019 Stiletto Contest hosted by Contemporary Romance Writers, a chapter of Romance Writers of America. Her novels are being translated into several languages.

When Lucia isn't writing, you can find her relaxing with her toes in the sand at a nearby beach. She runs on caffeine, scorching hot sunshine, and four hours of sleep. She's written nine books and has many more planned for the years to come.

Find out more at authorluciafranco.com.

Printed in Great Britain
by Amazon

79140500R00124